Finding  His Ranch

STAND-ALONE BOOK

A Christian Historical Romance Book

by

Chloe Carley

Disclaimer & Copyright

This is a work of fiction. Names, characters, places and incidents either are products of the author's imagination or are used fictitiously. Any resemblance to actual events or locales or persons, living or dead, is entirely coincidental.

Copyright© 2025 by Chloe Carley

All Rights Reserved.

This book may not be reproduced or transmitted in any form without the written permission of the publisher.

In no way is it legal to reproduce, duplicate, or transmit any part of this document in either electronic means or in printed format. Recording of this publication is strictly prohibited and any storage of this document is not allowed unless with written permission from the publisher.

Table of Contents

Disclaimer & Copyright...2

Table of Contents 3

Prologue 5

Chapter One 10

Chapter Two 18

Chapter Three..24

Chapter Four 30

Chapter Five 33

Chapter Six 36

Chapter Seven 44

Chapter Eight 50

Chapter Nine 57

Chapter Ten..63

Chapter Eleven 70

Chapter Twelve 75

Chapter Thirteen 78

Chapter Fourteen 85

Chapter Fifteen...92

Chapter Sixteen 102

Chapter Seventeen..110

Chapter Eighteen 119

Chapter Nineteen..129

Chapter Twenty 141

Chapter Twenty-One 149
Chapter Twenty-Two 155
Chapter Twenty-Three 162
Chapter Twenty-Four 173
Chapter Twenty-Five 178
Chapter Twenty-Six 185
Chapter Twenty-Seven 190
Chapter Twenty-Eight 199
Chapter Twenty-Nine 209
Chapter Thirty 215
Chapter Thirty-One 222
Epilogue 234
Extended Epilogue 238
Also, by Chloe Carley 254

Prologue

Springfield, Illinois, April 1890 ...

Ms. Annalise Owens stood hunched over a sink full of dishes as she scrubbed hard at a dirty cooking pot with the rough wash rag. She used her soaked forearm to push some of her dark hair out of her face and continued to scrub as she ignored a few drops of liquid that joined the soapy water. Although Annalise was working hard at her job, it wasn't her sweat that had fallen into the water, but her tears. Even the obnoxious sounds coming from the occupied section of the brothel couldn't distract Annalise from her thoughts. Her heart ached with a feeling of great sorrow as she thought of her mother who had passed away just three months prior. Oh, how Annalise wished that God's plan had not included that illness that took her mother far too soon, leaving her all alone to care for her five-year-old brother, Jamie.

The door to the kitchen slammed open and Annalise jumped in surprise, splashing water onto the front of her dress. In marched Madam Levoy. The older brothel manager always had her face painted and her grey hair pinned up in place. She wore intricate dresses that revealed more than Annalise was comfortable seeing, and today was no different. However, Madam's face was pinched much more than usual and her cheeks were flushed red. Behind her, she dragged along Jamie, his green eyes wide with shock and his lips pressed to avoid crying out as Madam's fingernails dug into his arm."

Just behind Jamie and Madam was Annalise's best friend Lucy, her light brown hair wavy hair falling out of its braid to border around her worried eyes and apologetic smile. She had some of her green dress pulled up and wound up in her hands to allow her to run after Madame. "I'm so sorry Annalise," Lucy said, out of breath and with a tremble of fear.

Madam's dark eyes drilled holes into Annalise, her mouth pinched until she spoke. "What is Lucy doing, watching over your charge? You're keeping her away from paying customers." Madam pulled Jamie around and released him towards Annalise. Annalise quickly pulled her small, thin brother into her arms and wrapped around him protectively.

Annalise's voice shook but her gaze met the Madam's. "All of the customers were already attended to when I asked Lucy to play with him outside. Young boys need room to run around so I thought-"

"You thought?" Madam replied with a snort through her nose. "I don't pay you to think. You're here to work and do as I say." Her glaring gaze lowered from Annalise down to Jamie. "There will be no more playing from you. I will not have anyone living off my business for free."

"He's only five," Annalise squeaked out, feeling as if her words were getting caught in her throat.

Madam continued, her haughty voice piercing out as her gaze returned to Annalise, "It's bad enough that you don't pull your weight here, but stopping Lucy from fulfilling her duties as well is unacceptable."

As she spoke, the Madam's voice grew louder until Annalise was sure that all the customers could hear her. Her shoulders turned inward and her line of sight fell to the floor even as she clutched her brother tightly. Although a righteous fire burned in her chest at the way she and Jamie were treated, she could not find any more words to speak.

The cruel brothel manager continued, only slightly appeased by Annalise's lack of response. "It's about time that you earn your keep. Washing dishes will no longer be enough. If you want to stay, start taking clients." She turned on her heel and left just as quickly as she had entered. As Madam's words fell upon her ears, Annalise felt all air leave her lungs. She looked up at Lucy and clung to the sight of her friend like a candlelight in the darkness. Her knees felt wobbly under her and she was sure that if it wasn't for Jamie's grasp, she would have already fallen down. She could never give up her body to a man that she wasn't married to. The Madam couldn't make her...could she? Everyone stood in stunned silence while Annalise's tears only rained down harder at the impossible choice that stood before her.

That night, after a long evening of soothing Jamie to sleep, Lucy and Annalise sat together as the candlelight flickered and cast shadows along the walls and Jamie's sleeping form. Lucy held her friend's hand as she tried to comfort her. "Please trust that God has a plan for you," she whispered.

Annalise stifled another sob with two hands across her mouth. Her shoulders shook with the effort to contain her emotions and she felt her chest tighten. When air returned to her lungs, she responded, her voice barely audible, "Why would He put me in this position then? I don't want to sleep with anyone unless I'm married to them. There's nowhere else for us to go, I can't let Jamie live on the streets." She could hardly keep her sobs muffled and she crouched down, nearly rolling up into a ball with her knees pulled up against her chest.

Lucy patted her back. "There are other options." She pulled out an advertisement that she had cut from the daily newspaper and held it out, waiting patiently. Annalise slowly unwrapped herself, wiped away a few tears, and took the paper, bringing it closer to the candlelight. She quickly read the top line: 'Mail Order Bride Wanted'.

Their gazes met and Annalise struggled to find words. "I can't marry some random man."

Lucy wrapped her friend in a hug, "But I want you to be happy. This is the way out." Annalise shook her head as she desperately tried to think of some other option. She had always wanted to meet someone, court, and fall in love. Someone she could create a family with. Someone she choose. Her stomach churned slightly at the idea of marrying the first man whose advertisement she found. "Don't make a decision tonight," Lucy said gently. "Get some rest." She patted her friend's hand and then left the room, heading to her own.

Once Lucy was gone, Annalise read through the article and thought through her options. Despite her friend's words ringing in her mind, she put the advertisement down, knowing that first thing in the morning, she would have to find a different solution. This was not the answer. Unable to get comfortable in her bed, she fell into a fitful rest, tossing and turning for a while before she relaxed into a deep sleep.

In her dream, Annalise wandered around a dark space as she desperately looked for something. Suddenly a bright white light flashed before her and there was a massive presence, as if the sun itself had stepped into the room with her. Annalise fell to her knees at the sight and feeling of the creature. She was sure that it could only be one thing: a magnificent angel. In a musical voice the angel spoke to her, "It is time to go. There is more waiting for you out in the world. Follow the road ahead."

Annalise woke with a start, the angel's words echoing through her mind. Without meaning to, she looked over to where she had set the advertisement down and felt a fire ignite in her chest. This was the only option to follow. She quickly relit her candle and pulled out some paper and ink at her small desk. She skimmed through the advertisement once more, noting that the country cattle rancher only wanted a wife to help him run and take of his property and workers. With a quick nod to herself, she got to work writing a reply. Her hands shook with nerves, but the words she penned were determined. This had to be God's plan for her.

Chapter One

Williamsville, Illinois, April 1890 ...

Reid Shaw stood with his hands on his hips, watching a wagon a few miles in the distance as it drove past his acres of cattle and land and towards where he stood at his main ranch house. Even from here with just a little squint of his eyes, Reid could see that it was his younger sister Polly by the look of the wagon and the way she drove.

He shook his head, the smallest of smiles resting on the corner of his mouth. He tilted his head down, allowing the worn cowboy hat to shield his release of emotion from the world. He wiped his hands on his jeans and then turned around and headed toward the barns to let his workers know that he would be unavailable until Polly was done visiting.

By the time Polly pulled her horse and wagon up to the main barn, Reid was out and waiting and he quickly took over after a small wave. She looked just the same as ever with her brown hair pulled up and pinned behind her head, the same golden eyes as him, and a kind, knowing smile. She had always had a very motherly aura, even before having kids. Reid had always assumed it was because their parents had died when she was so young and she had to fill that void.

He unhitched her horse and put it in a stall to eat food and drink water. As soon as he was back out of the stable, Polly wrapped him in a warm hug. "It's been a bit since I've seen you," he teased her.

Polly let out a louder than necessary sigh "George was able to take some time off to watch the children so I could get over here. I can't believe it's already been a month since I made the trip."

"You must have left early," Reid replied with a glance up at the sun. "It's not even noon yet."

"That's right," Polly nodded. She looked thoughtful for a moment. "I've found it's much easier to slip out of the house before everyone's really up and moving. Otherwise I get caught up with the children and then before I know it, the day has already passed me by."

"How are Catherine and Fredrick doing?" Reid asked as he thought fondly of his niece and nephew.

"Catherine is keeping us on our toes. She can pretty much walk anywhere now. She's really started to pick on Fredrick and won't give him any space or time alone with his books or toys." Polly chuckled, then shook her head. "Enough about me; how are things going on here? The ranch looks great from what I saw driving up." She looked around her childhood home, her face warm and relaxed. The siblings started walking towards the far pen where the largest pasture was visible.

"It's going well. Nearly all our calves made it through spring. We also just bought a few new bulls so they're getting acclimated with the herd over here." He pointed out a specific section of field that was fenced in by long wooden boards. "You want to take a ride and I can show you the new improvements on the east side of the property?" Polly nodded, already itching to get back in the saddle after her long drive, and they walked towards the horse pasture to get some geldings saddled up.

When they reached the fence line after they had fetched the halters, one of the newer ranch hands, Jeffery, noticed them and stopped his work, putting down the boards he was going to replace. "Miss, would you like a hand with that?" he offered kindly. The boy hadn't been working there long enough to remember Polly on sight, but he was very polite and waited patiently for a reply as he tucked his hands behind his back and made eye contact with them. His green eyes contrasted his very freckled face and red tinged hair.

Reid and Polly had a quick moment of eye contact before she turned and handed the halter to Jeffery. "I would appreciate that, thank you," she said, smiling warmly at him. Jeffery quickly hopped the fence and hurried to catch her a horse without a moment to lose.

"Don't want to catch your own horse?" Reid asked with a small smirk on his lips.

She gestured back towards where her horse was stabled. "I already did that today. Besides, the kind gentleman offered." Reid let out a chuckle and then climbed over the fence.

"Catch Sundance for her," he called out to Jeffery before going to collect his own horse, Lycan. He found his blue roan towards the back of the field as it grazed on a nice patch of green grass shielded from the sun by some large oak trees. The large horse had a dark gray, almost black, mane and tail. Its coat was a light gray color that nearly looked blue with slightly darker gray spots along its back and sides. Reid let out a familiar whistle and Lycan nickered a greeting in return. After a few more bites of grass, Lycan stood patiently as Reid slipped the halter over his head. Reid provided his horse with a few neck pats and some scratches on the top part of his face and then Lycan followed Reid back over to the top of the pasture.

They exited the field and once Reid had the gate secured behind them, they headed to the tack shed.

Reid tied his horse and then quickly got his bridle, saddle blanket, and saddle on and cinched up. He mounted and comfortably rode Lycan out to where Polly was waiting on the brown gelding Sundance. She was giving her mount a few pats on the back and ruffles to his mane. Seeing Reid, she smiled mischievously, "What took you so long? Sundance and I were ready to get started without you."

"Sundance never leaves the front half of the pasture. Lycan loves the back," he said defensively before he patted his horse affectionately. Before Polly could reply, Reid urged his horse forward and they took off, shooting down the dirt road towards the far pastures. Reid glanced back and could see that after a moment of surprise, Polly urged her horse along, running fast to catch up with them. They raced to the far end of the property, just as they used to do as kids, before they slowed down to give their horses a rest and give themselves a chance to talk.

"You got a major head start back there," Polly said, her voice carrying some feigned hurt.

Reid smiled slightly and immediately changed the subject. "The last time you were here, we'd started replacing all these fences. Since then, we finished that project. While we were digging, we noticed a few spots of spring water. So, we started a few wells and have been using them to provide more water on this side of the property for the cattle."

"I thought you and Father had searched on this side of the property and were never able to find any water other than Rush

Creek a few miles away," Polly said, raising an eyebrow in thought.

Reid's face crumpled slightly. A storm cloud seated itself on his mind at the mention of their father. "Well, we never found any. But there's water here now." He nudged his heels into the side of his horse and started walking back towards the main part of the property. Polly quickly followed him and allowed the topic to change.

"Have you gotten the grain storage container fixed up? You're going to need that come this fall," she said in a knowing voice.

Reid let out a sigh. "We replaced all the rusty sections, but honestly it would do a lot better if we just rebuilt the whole thing. It's been here forever, and seems to do more harm than good these days."

"Do you have money in the budget to make that happen?"

"Well..." Reid rubbed the back of his neck. "Sure... if I hadn't just bought that new herd of cattle and the new plow. We won't be making that money back until the end of fall when we sell off some of the livestock. And by then, I just don't know if we'll have the time to put a new structure in place before frost starts setting in." Polly shook her head in agreement, knowing that making decisions for a ranch was always going to be tough.

They continued their tour, making their way around the ranch as Reid showed Polly all the other things that had changed since her last visit. She turned to him as they were heading back. "I'm really proud of you; the ranch looks even more successful than the last time I visited. And it always seems to be the talk of the town." He glanced away at the unexpected compliment but nodded his head in thanks. They soon headed back to the tack shed to rub down their mounts and release them back into the pasture. Just before Reid let Lycan go, he gave him and Sundance a sugar cube through the fence, and then he and Polly made their way over to the house.

Reid's house was simple and clean, furnished the same as it had been before his sister had moved out after marrying George. Truthfully, Reid spent so much time outside the house that the building's only purpose to him was a place to sometimes sleep and sometimes eat. During the summer he spent so much time sleeping outside and cooking on fires that his house wasn't used that much. In the kitchen, he scrambled to make food and settled on some bread and cheese with some peach preserves that had been canned since the previous summer. He got everything plated and brought it over to the table where Polly was waiting. His sister glanced at the simple meal and shook her head a little. "So, when are you planning on getting a wife?"

He stopped his bread just a few inches from his mouth as his sister asked the dreaded question. He placed his food back down with a sigh and a wish that the conversation was already over. "I like my independence," he replied simply. His lone wolf status was something that he had always prided himself on. Polly remained silent for a moment, and Reid quickly took a few bites, digging into the food. He was almost giddy at the thought that Polly might have let the subject drop.

To his disappointment, however, she started again in a soft voice that held a lot of sympathy. "You can't let the bad things in your past harm your chances of a great future." Reid remained quiet and continued to eat, actively ignoring her statement.

Polly took a few bites of her food. "Surely there are some local women you might be interested in? From what I've seen in church, there are quite a few single ladies in town looking for an eligible bachelor." Reid's ears rang, but she continued to talk. "I know that it's hard to meet people when you're always out here on the ranch, but I'm sure I could set up some correspondence with a few of the ladies for you. That way you could at least talk to them and try to see if you would be interested in any of them. There's this one lovely lady named Victoria who-"

"I submitted an ad in the paper," Reid interrupted quickly to stop his sister from carrying on. She paused and glanced at him in surprise.

She seemed not to believe him as she asked carefully, "An ad?"

"For a mail-order bride," he explained in a slightly embarrassed tone.

"You submitted an ad," Polly repeated, her voice raising an octave as she hopped up to her feet in giddy energy. He looked down at his plate and continued eating, almost wishing that he hadn't interrupted her. "Have you had any responses? When did the paper run? Oh my goddess, this is so exciting!"

"Well, I actually accepted someone already," he continued slowly.

Polly jumped back into her chair and leaned hard against the table toward him. "You accepted someone? Tell me everything." Reid thought her voice sounded similar to a tweeting bird since she had been caught up in the excitement.

"Her name is Annalise," he offered. "We exchanged letters a few times and she's from Springfield. She accepted my offer and I sent the fare for her travels. She'll be arriving at the train station on Friday."

"Friday?" Polly chirped out and hopped up from her chair once more. "Why that's just later this week." She fell back down into her chair, her mouth open slightly in shock.

Reid shrugged his shoulders and began to defend his decision to his surprised sister. "I need more help. Just like I hire a ranch hand to help with the cattle, I need a… wife to help me with making the food and taking care of the house. Everything is just becoming a lot to handle on my own so, I finally took your advice."

Polly took his hand into her own and smiled at him as if her heart was going to burst open with happiness. "I very much look forward to meeting her. Friday will be here before we know it." While Polly's voice was filled with joy, a sense of unease filled Reid's chest at the thought of Annalise's arrival in just a few days. His whole life was going to be different, but he wasn't sure yet if it would truly be for the better.

Chapter Two

April 1890 ...

Annalise stood on the train station platform. Jamie's hand was gripped tightly in her own. In her other hand was the newspaper ad, a letter from Reid, and a letter from Lucy. At her feet were two bags of luggage in tattered suitcases. She was wearing her very best dress, a lilac hoop skirt that was a little worn down, but in much better condition than anything else she owned. Her dark hair was pinned up, although she knew it was a little unruly from the travel.

Annalise glanced around the small train station, watching the few other travelers walk about. Jamie and she had boarded the train in Springfield and after just a few stops they had arrived in Williamsville where Mr. Reid Shaw lived. She glanced at his letter once more and checked for the fifteenth time that she had taken the correct train, had gotten off at the correct station, and had stopped to wait at the correct spot.

She hoped that she looked calm on the outside because inside, a terrifying fear coursed through her veins. She hadn't told the rancher in her letters that she had Jamie with her. She had been so afraid that he wouldn't accept her because of it. It wasn't every day that a mail-order bride advertisement showed up. If she had waited for one that was asking for the bride to already have children in their care, she would have never made it out of the brothel. A sick feeling swarmed her stomach when she remembered writing back to Mr. Shaw and leaving out Jamie. A good, God-fearing woman should never lie to anyone, let alone the man she was trying to marry. She put a hand over her mouth in an attempt to hold back the bile that was starting to rise.

Her only hope was that he would have pity on her and take them anyway, despite her withholding information. She prayed that Mr. Shaw would meet her and Jamie and realize that it was a good decision to go through with, even if it was a surprise. The thought of him rejecting her and sending them back home caused her hands to shake slightly.

Not only was she afraid of what the rancher might do, but she could feel nervousness bundling up in her chest at this new venture, away from everything she had ever known. She had never left the city. Had never really left the brothel much either. But she couldn't have stayed there and been forced to do something she didn't believe in. The madam had given her no choice.

Annalise thought back to the times when her mother had talked about the future and all of the good things she wanted for her children. She had always reminded her daughter to trust in God and the journey that he had planned for her. *Oh Lord, please look out for Jamie and me*, she prayed quickly.

"When can we go home?" Jamie's small voice interrupted her spiraling thoughts.

Annalise kneeled down beside her brother, careful not to get her dress dirty. "We're going to a new home, remember?" She re-tucked in his shirt and straightened his clothes before sliding her fingers through his hair to get it all in order.

"I don't want to be here," Jamie said. His bottom lip pushed forward and he stomped his foot on the ground before he hunched his back over slightly. Annalise took a breath and examined her brother, trying to understand the reasons behind his actions. She thought back to their last meal, many hours before when the sun had not even started to rise. How they had sat on the uncomfortable train seats and Jamie had not been able to nap or even play much since the day before. She glanced around the station and could just make out a restaurant and store that were down the street. The thought of food caused her stomach to contract, and she imagined Jamie's must be doing so as well. A quick pat of her pocket, however, held only bad news. There was no jangle of coins left. All of their money was gone, used up to get them out there.

She bit her lip in worry before she wrapped her brother up in a hug. "God has a plan for us. I'm sure that our new home will be so lovely and have plenty of space for you to run and play. I know that you've only ever been in the city, but I hear that in the country there are a lot of trees and grass and rocks, and sticks, and plenty of fun things for you to get into." Jamie smiled slightly at that thought. She patted his cheek gently before standing up and looking around them once more.

Mr. Shaw had not told her in the letter how she would identify him at the train station, and while she was sure that she stuck out, standing off to the side with their bags, obviously waiting on someone, she didn't know how she would find him without him identifying her first. She smiled at the few people who walked by, but no one stopped or tried to speak with her. "Let's play a game," she said suddenly to her brother.

"What kind of game?" he asked, already sounding less upset.

Annalise looked around the train station. "There sure are a lot of signs all around. Do you recognize any of the letters?" Jamie's lips pinched together as he focused on the words of the nearby signs.

Finally, after a moment of concentration, he spoke, "Right there is an 'r'."

"That's correct," she congratulated. "Now, how many letter 'r's can you find? Go ahead and count how many you see on all the signs." He began to count quietly to himself, moving his fingers as he went.

Annalise used the moment to glance at the letters in her hand again, this time reading through the one from Lucy. In the weeks since Lucy had discovered the ad and shown it to her, she had been such a strong supporter of Annalise. Her friend had helped her read through Mr. Shaw's responses and write new letters. It had been Annalise's idea to leave out the part about Jamie, but Lucy had agreed that it might be for the best not to mention to it until she absolutely had to. It was their understanding that most men did not want to take in children who were not their own.

Annalise had already read the goodbye letter so many times on the train that she had the words memorized. But still, she allowed her gaze to drift over the letter. It was a goodbye note, one that Lucy had placed by her bed before she had left that morning. It read, *My dearest friend, I am so happy that you are able to follow the path that God has made for you. You are so strong and courageous to bring Jamie and yourself on this journey. I will miss you terribly and can hardly stand the thought of not being with you, but I'm glad that you are able to get out of here and start your life. Write to me often, I will be awaiting your first letter to hear how everything went and is going. Love and prayers, Lucy.*

Reading the letter gave Annalise a small boost of bravery. She glanced around the station again, still seeing no one who looked like a rancher. However, one of the train station employees was walking along the platform. The older gentleman was smartly dressed in his navy uniform, his hair slicked back and his posture proper. If anyone on this platform could identify the rancher for her, it might be him. She quickly flagged him down and he stopped beside her. "I'm sorry, but I'm looking for someone. Do you happen to know a Mr. Shaw?"

The employee glanced around, and the spectacles on his nose slid down slightly. He pushed them back up before he quickly shook his head. "I'm sorry Miss, but it's been a while since I've seen him around this area."

"Oh, okay. Thank you," she replied, trying not to sound disappointed.

"Good day, Miss," the employee said before continuing slowly on his path.

"There are twelve letter 'r's," Jamie said with some excitement.

"That's wonderful counting," Annalise complimented. "You even kept all your numbers in order." Jamie beamed up to her with pride. "What letter would you like to count now?"

He tapped his finger on his chin in thought. "How about the letter 'a'?"

"Very well. Go ahead and get started," Annalise told him. He started to quietly count to himself once more.

She looked around the station once more, wondering if something could have happened to Mr. Shaw's wagon or if there was a problem at his ranch that had delayed his arrival. She began to worry less about him rejecting her and more about him not showing up at all. She had no money left and no place to go. What would she do? It was bad enough that she had to take care of herself on no money, but with Jamie as well, it was going to be near impossible if Mr. Shaw never came for them. Annalise continued scanning the area when an unfamiliar man stepped up to the platform. She turned toward him and quickly noticed his old and dirty clothes that hung on his tall and muscled body. His boots were crusted with mud, and his hat looked older than Jamie. Although his clothes were dirty, he himself seemed well kept, with clean hands and a neatly trimmed beard that helped to square his jaw. Just under his hat, she could see brown hair, but what amazed her were his bright golden eyes.

As the rancher slowly approached her, he looked at her with a slight air of friendly openness. But then his gaze dropped to Jamie by her side, and everything in his demeanor changed to surprised betrayal. Oh, no.

Chapter Three

Reid made eye contact with the only unaccompanied female on the entire platform. He did his best not to immediately dismiss her, although her fancy purple dress did not put him at ease. He wondered if she could be any good at being a rancher's wife if she wasn't willing or able to get dirty and work hard. He did his best to breathe through his emotions, though, knowing what Polly would say.

When he looked past the dress, what he saw caused his heart to skip a beat, and any words he might have said became caught in his throat. She was beautiful, with brilliant green eyes and the darkest hair which was mostly pinned up. A few loose strands fell down along the side of her face and curled around, only serving to draw him in. Her high cheekbones held a bit of a rosy hue and he found himself worrying if she might be getting too hot. Then their gazes met, and he felt as if she could see through him to his soul. The best kind of look you'd want to have from someone you were going to be spending the rest of your life with.

But then he saw a little boy standing beside her. Anger and distrust flared in his chest, and his teeth clenched together. She had said nothing about a child in her letters. She had only made it very clear that she had never been married and never been with a man. Yet, here she was, with a child.

He forced himself to take a few deep breaths and continued to walk, although at a much slower pace now. He glanced around the platform as his nerves worked themselves through his stomach. A train was just pulling out of the station, the noise of its engine and whistle drowned out all other sounds on the platform. The connecting rods moved the wheels and slowly turned them faster.

The train headed off as it followed the tracks and chugged along to its next destination. He winced slightly at the sound. Although he often heard the train from a distance, he had rarely had a reason to go to the station and hear its chorus this close. And since he planned to live on his ranch in the mountains for the rest of his life, he doubted that he would see the train this close again very much in the future.

The unaccompanied woman and the child remained where they were, even as everyone else on the platform dispersed. The people either headed into the nearby businesses or left the platform altogether with friends or family. When he was within a few feet of the woman, he stopped and awkwardly looked between her and the little boy who hadn't even noticed him, as he seemed to be eagerly reading the signs around the train station while he counted on his fingers. "Excuse me, but are you Miss Annalise Owens?" he asked.

"Yes, I am," the young lady responded. "Are you Mr. Reid Shaw?"

A lump formed in his throat and he swallowed hard. "Yes, ma'am. I am." Reid then felt his companion's presence just behind him. He stepped over slightly to allow room for Wade to stand beside him.

They all stood in a momentary silence before Wade tipped his hat at Miss Owens. "I'm Wade Barnes, Ma'am…I'm Reid's…" he glanced at Reid for a moment before he finished his sentence, "…foreman."

"It's nice to meet you both." Annalise gave them a curtsey. Reid couldn't help but feel slightly smitten by the lovely woman in front of him, yet every time he caught sight of the young boy, the heat of anger returned to his chest. Silence fell over the group once more and finally the little boy looked up at them, noticing the strangers. The child stepped behind Annalise and pulled on her skirt nervously as he eyed the two men. Reid wondered if the boy felt just how uncomfortable the silence was that surrounded them.

At the thoughts of the boy, Reid clenched his fists tightly at his sides, trying to contain the frustration that bubbled up inside of him. When Wade nudged his shoulder, he nearly boiled over. His gaze cut to his friend.

"Will you give us just a moment?" Wade said apologetically to Annalise, not even looking at Reid before he dragged him away from the open platform and toward the closest building which was a small general store. Reid allowed himself to be pulled but he didn't make it easy on Wade as he didn't appreciate that he took control of the situation when it really wasn't his place.

They stopped just out of earshot and Reid looked begrudgingly at Wade, not daring to glance back at his mail-order bride and her child. Wade took off his hat and ran his fingers through his blond hair as he shook his head. "Boss, you gotta talk to her."

Reid simply glared at his best friend. He didn't have to talk to anybody. Not if he didn't want to.

Wade sighed. "I know that she wasn't supposed to have a kid, but she did travel here and leave everything behind to be with you. That's got to count for something."

"Not everything," Reid finally said before he clenched his teeth together.

"What?" Wade tilted his head to the side.

"She didn't leave everything behind."

A puff of air escaped Wade's lips and he wiped at his face in an irritated fashion before he put his hat back on. "Just go talk to her. Give her a chance to explain the situation. If things don't go well, we can send her back. But at least talk to her. She isn't Laura, you know."

Reid's golden eyes narrowed; his lips pressed into a tight line. He turned around and headed back to Miss Owens, stopping a few feet short of her. She looked at him with her green eyes wide and innocent looking, as if she had no sins to atone for. He glanced down at her lips and wondered briefly what it would be like to kiss them. Words tumbled around Reid's head as he tried to figure out what to say, but then his gaze landed on the boy. In a low and cold voice, he spoke, his eyes once again trained on Miss Owens. "I asked for a wife, not a ready-made family."

Annalise's head recoiled as if she had been struck and her body stiffened. Reid felt a slight pang of regret in his chest because he had caused her pain, but he continued to speak, only knowing his words once they had left his mouth. "I'm going to talk with the agency to cancel this marriage. You can be on the next train back as soon as tomorrow." He started to turn, ready to leave her and all this ridiculousness behind, but then Annalise fell to her knees, her purple dress swooshing onto the wooden floor, causing some dirt to powder the air. Her sudden movement startled him and he stepped backward in surprise while also starting to lean forward to help her up. Her words caused him to freeze in place with her still at his feet, the edge of her dress just touching his dirt-covered boots.

"Please don't send us back," she begged. It sounded as if she was choking on her words. They seemed to get stuck in her throat but still, she forced them out, even as her eyes became watery and her clenched hands, which were knotted up in her dress, started to tremble. "If we return, I'll be forced into a life I can't bear, and Jamie will suffer. If you have any kindness in your heart, give us refuge."

Reid looked at the poor woman and felt his heart soften. She looked so sad and alone. Just her and a child against the world. It reminded him of himself, standing in the empty ranch house at thirteen with just his younger sister beside him. All the mourners had left, and in their place were many dishes of food, many bouquets of flowers, and two fresh graves with the dirt not even fully settled on top of them. He remembered the feeling of having no one to rely on except himself. Having to take care of someone else. Having no one to turn to.

Even as he felt sympathy flood his heart, he was still wary. She had never mentioned the child in her letters. His mind started to spiral and he felt sweat gather on his body. Perhaps there was more she was hiding. She might be trying to take advantage of him. It was his policy not to trust people, and now was not the time to start. He extended his hands and quickly helped her back up to her feet. He felt a tinge of embarrassment that she had begged on her knees to him, and he hoped that no one else, other than Wade and the child, had seen that. "I can't marry a woman who already has a child," he said firmly but softly. In his mind, he willed her to understand that this result was not his fault but her own.

"Jamie isn't mine," Annalise insisted immediately before she quickly wiped away a tear that was starting to streak down her face. "I have never been with a man. I believe that that should be something that is reserved for a man and his wife as God intended." He frowned at the mention of God's intentions. Annalise saw the change on his face and begged again, "Trust me, please."

Chapter Four

Annalise's heart pounded wildly in her chest as she waited for Mr. Shaw to respond. He continued to stare at her with his golden eyes as he looked to be in deep concentration. She wondered if he could ever forgive her for withholding that she was bringing Jamie. At the time, it had seemed like the best option, but now she wondered if perhaps he would have responded better if she had been more upfront with him. However, when she examined his grumpy face which contrasted with his earlier positive expression when seeing her, she figured that he probably wouldn't have responded better because he wouldn't have responded to her letters at all.

She glanced behind him at where Mr. Barnes, the foreman, stood. His blue eyes met hers with a kindness that she had yet to receive from anyone else since starting on this journey, although his expression was also filled with a mixture of pity and worry. She continued to glance toward the foreman, doing her best to beg with her eyes rather than her words this time. She hoped that Mr. Barnes would encourage Mr. Shaw to keep her and Jamie. She had nowhere else to go, and she would not return to the brothel. This was her only option.

Suddenly a different voice cut through the silence. "Now that's no way to talk to a lady." Everyone turned to see who it was. It was then that Annalise saw the large, portly man approaching them. It seemed like he had been watching them from a shadowy area beside one of the nearby businesses. She wondered, with a slight flush of embarrassment, how long he had been observing them. As he walked up to them, she quickly stood and brushed her hands down the front of her dress, hoping that it was still clean enough.

The man seemed to be older than all the adults present with a thick beard and brown hair that had become thin toward the back. His button-down shirt, jeans, and boots were clean and fancy. While he was much neater than Mr. Shaw and Mr. Barnes, the man's clothes were of the same style as them. Annalise wondered if he also had a ranch, but just didn't work it himself.

Chin up, head held high, and with wide, self-assured steps, he carried himself with an air of confidence that a president or sheriff might be expected to have. His squinty brown eyes scanned Annalise and Jamie in an almost hungry fashion before he turned toward Mr. Shaw. Annalise couldn't help but shiver slightly and she felt that she and Jamie should get as far away from this man as possible. But despite that feeling, she remained rooted in place, only clenching Jamie tighter against her side.

The man stopped in front of Mr. Shaw in a friendly manner and put his hands on his hips. "Now Reid, I couldn't help but overhear that you were about to send this lovely woman home." Mr. Shaw glared at him, but the man continued to speak, undeterred. "I would be happy to take the girl off your hands. My ranch is growing so large. I could always use some more help in the kitchen or with the cleaning." He spread his hands wide. "The boy could be trained quickly as a ranch hand. I have no doubt about that."

Annalise bristled at his words and red anger started to cloud her vision. The man continued to talk, not bothering to glance her way.

"I'd be happy to reimburse you for whatever you paid to the agency to make it worth your while."

Fear clung to Annalise's heart as she worried that the man's deal might be too good for Mr. Shaw to pass up. The agency on their own would probably not give Mr. Shaw his money back, but this man was willing to purchase Jamie and her from him. A tiny feeling inside of her screamed for her to get away from this man. He wasn't safe. While she didn't mind being put to work in the kitchen or with the cleaning, she would not allow Jamie to work at the young age of five. That was unacceptable.

Her hands shook as she spoke, her voice loud and clear, "I am not an item to be sold or thrown around, and neither is Jamie."

The large man turned to look at her, his eyes narrowed slightly in anger at her statement. He turned his body fully away from Mr. Shaw and Mr. Barnes to look at her, his large stature immediately towered over her. His gaze seemed to be filled with ice. Although Annalise trembled, she stood her ground and did not lower her eyes.

Chapter Five

As soon as Carter Johnson showed up and his annoying voice started to grate against Reid's ears, Reid's blood began to boil and every square inch of his body was on high alert. Carter had proved time and time again in the past that he was nothing but trouble, and this time would be no different. Reid understood the game and he knew that he had to win this. He would do everything in his power to make sure that Carter never won again.

As Carter started to talk about Miss Owens and the child like they were property to be bargained for, Reid felt his skin start to grow hot. He prepared a retort, but before he could speak, Miss Owens did, standing up for herself and the boy. Reid froze in surprise and he quickly realized just how impressed he was of her for doing so. It wasn't often that a woman would stand up to a man, let alone a man she didn't know in a strange place that she had never been.

He immediately followed her lead and stepped between her and Carter, turning himself into a human shield. "You heard the lady. Mind your own business, Carter. This does not concern you."

He held up his hands in mock surrender, "I was only trying to help," he explained before the corner of his lip turned up in a nasty smile. "After all, I have experience caring for your leftovers."

Reid lunged for Carter, letting his fists loose as they aimed for his head. Wade grabbed Reid around his middle, just barely holding him back, nearly causing them to fall down. Carter moved away but not in a hurried or worried manner. He took his time, the smirk still locked on his face as he made his way down the platform. He tipped his hat towards Miss Owens and continued walking.

"He's not worth it, you know this is what he wants," Wade said sternly to Reid. He nearly spoke the words right into his ears, so as Carter wouldn't overhear him. Reid shook Wade off and stood in place, his body vibrating. His chest heaved and his heart pumped wildly as he watched his rival walk away without a deserved black eye.

He tore his gaze away from Carter and turned swiftly back to Miss Owens. "Come with me," he said as he snatched up her suitcase and spun back around. Their arms nearly made contact as he passed, and a wild array of emotions swirled in his chest at her closeness. He shook it off and continued walking at a quick pace down the platform in the opposite direction of Carter, back towards where his wagon was waiting. He glanced back a few times to check that she was keeping up. Every time, he saw what looked like terror on her face with her green eyes wide and her skin incredibly pale. The boy began to cry loudly as Miss Owens pulled him along in an attempt to keep up with Reid. Wade took up the rear and followed close behind. The walk down the platform seemed to be much quicker this time around. The businesses zoomed by, and none of them came close to claiming his attention.

Reid did his best to avoid eye contact with anyone they passed. They all stared at his group with hardly concealed curiosity. They seemed to look in astonishment at the strange party made up of an angry man, a terrified woman, a crying child, and a silent man. Although the boy continued to cry loudly, Reid did not stop as he passed the last boarding house and rounded the corner to the hitching post where his covered wagon was tied. He pulled the door open roughly and threw their luggage into the wagon as he waited impatiently for Miss Owens and the boy to arrive.

"This is just a trial," he said in a low and firm voice. Her green eyes met his. "You'll work at the ranch as a housekeeper until the trial period is finished. If things don't work out, I'll send you back to where you came from." His voice left no room for negotiation as he knew that he held all the cards.

Miss Owen's lips remained pinched together, although some of the color returned to her face. She quickly nodded her understanding before she began to help the boy up into the wagon. Reid quickly jumped into the driver's seat and waited impatiently for everyone else to be ready. Wade shut the wagon door behind Miss Owens and then quickly untied the horses. He climbed up to the front seat with Reid and grabbed the reins. With a quick shake, they were off and headed down the dirt path, leaving the town behind.

Wade continued to look straight ahead but spoke only loud enough for Reid to hear, "With a woman and child in the house, you're going to have to start controlling that temper." His voice held a twinge of amusement in it. Reid simply scowled.

Chapter Six

That evening, Annalise stood at the unfamiliar stove and worked to create a roast for all the men on the ranch. She already had some vegetables and meat in the large pan, and it sat heating up on the stove. She stood at the counter just off to the side and was cutting up more carrots to add to the mixture. The stove was a newer model and therefore wasn't similar to the one she had worked with at the brothel. Mr. Shaw had left her to it with only the barest of instructions on how anything worked or where to find any of the food.

She had been forced to scamper around to find what she needed. She dug through the cabinets, searched for the root cellar, and messed with the ice box until she was able to accumulate what she hoped would be enough food for all the working men. Annalise had never made this much food before at one time and she was more than a little nervous.

She set up a cutting board for Jamie to use at the counter and gave him the dullest knife she could find. After a small demonstration, she allowed Jamie to cut the potatoes. They worked together in silence for a while as the sounds of chops and clicks filled the air. After he helped cut up some potatoes and with nothing else to do at, Jamie became bored and slipped away from the cutting board to rummage through Mr. Shaw's cabinets.

"Oh no," Annalise said. "Let's leave that all alone…Grab some toys and go play quietly at the table." She continued working on the food as she spoke with him.

"But I want to go outside," Jamie whined. Annalise sympathized with how Jamie felt. They had gone from being stuffed inside a train to being stuffed inside a wagon. She also wanted some time to relax and stretch out the aches and pains of travel. She thought back to when they had left Springfield and were waiting outside the train station to be taken to Williamsville. Lucy had walked them there and after they exchanged hugs, she had left them because she was due back at the brothel and couldn't stay away long.

After they stood for a bit, Jamie started to get antsy. With reluctance, Annalise had allowed him to run around and play with his toys for a bit. He had chased some birds and dug in the ground with sticks. He had collected stones and searched for coins along the ground. That had been his last time playing outside. Now his whole world had turned upside down and he hadn't gotten a chance yet to even play outside in this new place.

"After dinner, perhaps we can go for a short walk outside, if Mr. Shaw agrees. But for now, I need you to behave and stay in sight. Go play at the table." She gestured for him to head in that direction. Jamie let out a sigh but moved to the other room. The dining room was connected to the kitchen by an arched doorway and while there were doors that could be shut between the two rooms, it looked like it had been many years since they had moved from their open position. The kitchen was stuffed with equipment, counters, and cabinets with a bit of floral wallpaper trimmed along the top edge of the walls. The dining room, however, was quite different. It was a spacious room with a large rectangular table in the center. Big windows let in the sun along the east side of the room. A few delicate paintings of cattle out in green pastures adorned the walls.

Jamie hauled himself up into a chair at the table and pulled some of his toys out of his pockets. Amongst them was his toy train. He began to run his train back and forth, making it zoom across the wood top of the table. Annalise winced, hoping that his playing wouldn't ruin it, but she allowed him to continue as she turned back to the kitchen to focus on dinner.

She continued chopping up the last of the vegetables as her mind retraced through the wild day they had experienced. The train ride, the strange Carter man, Mr. Shaw allowing them to stay with him-- for now. The wagon ride to the ranch had taken them farther up the mountain than Annalise had expected. While the city wasn't much different from where she had grown up, other than it being larger, she was so amazed to see the country from a closer vantage point than what the train had provided. It was nothing but trees, farmland, and some ranches as far as her eyes could see.

The roads were bumpy and uneven, but the wagon horse seemed to know what it were doing. She had been briefly worried about running into outlaws, but they only passed a few other carts and horse riders who did not interact with them. She couldn't hear Mr. Shaw or Mr. Barnes speak the entire ride, so she had spoken gentle words to Jamie, helping to calm him down. "We're headed to our new home now. Mr. Shaw will be taking care of us. It'll be a wonderful new start for us," she had explained to him. He had frowned at her words, not seeming to quite believe her. Eventually, he drifted off to sleep, his head leaned up against her shoulder as she did her best to hold it in place, especially when they hit potholes in the road.

Before she could see out the windows that they had arrived, she'd heard the horses call out to some friends. The wagon slowed its pace, then she and Jamie were quickly hurried out. Mr. Shaw walked them immediately to the large house at the center of the ranch, carrying their bags with him. Once inside, he hardly explained that she should get started on dinner before he disappeared again.

The smell of overcooked meat and charred vegetables tore her thoughts back to the present. She hurried over to the large pan and saw there wasn't enough liquid for the amount of food. The stove was heating it much too quickly for it to roast properly. Dark gray smoke started to curl out from the pan. Annalise swatted it away and quickly turned down the heat.

She hurried and got some water from the pail and added it to the pan. Sizzling erupted and more steam and smoke went up into the air. She quickly scraped at the bottom of the pan with a wooden spoon, trying to keep the food from burning more, all the while tears building up in the corners of her eyes, nothing to do with the smoke. All the commotion alerted Jamie and he appeared in the doorway. Seeing the smoke, he began to scream, "Fire! Fire!" in loud repetition.

"No, Jamie, it's okay," Annalise said, trying to soothe him while she scraped at the bottom of the pan. "It's just some smoke, everything is alright." She fumbled with the spoon and had to quickly retrieve it from the pan, the hot stick scalding her hand slightly. Her soothing sounds started to increase in volume and quickly became less soothing as Jamie's screaming flustered her.

The damage was already done though. Mr. Barnes appeared in the doorway with a large, heavy blanket and quickly pushed passed Jamie, ready to put out flames. He stopped in confusion when he only saw the slightly steamy pan with just a hint of burnt smell in the air. Mr. Shaw arrived just after him, and the concern on his face quickly changed to anger.

"What are you doing?" he asked. He pushed past the foreman to examine the pan. "Do you even know how to cook? Or were you lying about that as well?" His eyebrows hung darkly over his eyes and his bearded jaw was clenched.

Annalise bristled at the accusation. Her own mother had started to teach her how to cook just as soon as she could walk. She had put more hours of her life into cooking than anything else, except for maybe cleaning. "Of course I can cook," she said, her voice filled with ice. She became snappy. "But I've never cooked at this stove, with this equipment.

And I've never made such a large quantity of food. It might take me a moment to get used to things, but that doesn't mean that you get to question my abilities and call me a liar." Even as she said the words, she recognized the trouble she was in. Speaking hatefully to the man providing her with a home was never a smart move, especially one with a temper. Mr. Shaw looked like he had swallowed a storm cloud and bolts of lightning were going to shoot from his ears.

Mr. Barnes' eyes grew wide and he let out an awkward laugh before growing surer of himself as he gained their momentary attention. "You know, my mama was the best cook that I ever knew, and she burned something at least once a week. It's just part of the process," he said, waving off the incident as if it was no big deal. Mr. Shaw still didn't say anything, even as frustration seemed to come off of him in waves. He then turned and left the room, which caused the tension to immediately decrease. Mr. Barnes gave her a small smile, skirted Jamie, and left the room as well.

Annalise felt like crumpling to the floor, but instead, she grasped tightly onto the countertop and quickly said a prayer. "Bring me strength to make it through this. To help me survive this trial." As if answering her prayers, Jamie came over and wrapped his sister's legs in a large hug. She hugged him back and kissed his head before she shooed him back to his toys in the next room. She turned back to the stove and worked on getting more liquid in the pot after getting out the most burnt pieces of the strew so that it wouldn't mess up the flavor too much.

After she added the last of the vegetables and all the seasonings and spices, it was clear that the stew would be just fine, despite the mishap. She messed with the knob of the stove for a bit before she settled on a good temperature.

"Jamie," she called out as she started to pull out plates and silverware. Jamie appeared, looking a little disappointed to be needed. "Can you please set the table?" she asked.

"Okay," he agreed. Annalise was careful to only give him what his little arms could easily carry and after a few trips, he had brought everything to the table. They then both got to work to distribute everything at each seat. The last thing they added were the cloth napkins. It was then that the ranch hands began to file into the house, the noise from their conversations making the house much louder than it had been previously. With embarrassment and shyness, Annalise quickly finished up her placement of the napkins and then hurried Jamie and herself to the kitchen with his toys stuffed back into his pockets. To her disappointment, the men quickly followed her. They carried their plates to the pan and began to dish up food for themselves. They noticed her and Jamie and their conversations all seemed to pause. They nodded respectfully before heading back to the table, ready to eat and resume talking.

Mr. Shaw and Mr. Barnes were the last to enter the kitchen. Mr. Shaw mostly ignored her while Mr. Barnes smiled and handed two plates from the table to her. Annalise immediately realized that Mr. Barnes meant that Jamie and she were supposed to eat dinner with the rest of the group. Her cheeks grew hot and she started to stutter, trying to find her words. At the brothel, they had never eaten with the clients. Mr. Barnes quickly stopped her. "Everyone eats together," he explained simply. Annalise fell quiet and waited until the two men had left the kitchen before she dished up her and Jamie's food.

Annalise carried both plates and they entered the dining room. She was surprised to see where the two open seats were located. Mr. Barnes sat on one side of Mr. Shaw, but the two chairs on the other side of him were empty. It seemed like the cattle hands had left those for her and Jamie. She gulped and felt as if she was no longer hungry. With a deep breath, she headed towards the seats and placed herself beside Mr. Shaw with Jamie next to her. Nerves danced in her stomach and she could hardly keep her hands from shaking due to her being so close to him.

Once everyone was seated, the cattle hands lifted their forks to start eating. "Wait," Annalise interrupted. A few of them looked irritated but she quickly explained, "We need to say a blessing over the food."

Silence fell amongst everyone but the cattle hands shrugged their shoulders and bowed their heads, Mr. Barnes and Jamie joining in. Only Mr. Shaw remained upright, his head unbowed and his eyes open. Annalise hesitated for a moment before starting the blessing. She recognized that he was going to do what he wanted to do. "O Lord, bless us and this food. Thank

You for all of Your mercies that we receive. May we never stray from you. Through Jesus Christ, we pray, amen."

"Amen," the men repeated, before quickly digging into their food. While Jamie, Mr. Shaw, and herself were quiet while eating, everyone else seemed to laugh and joke in between bites of food and the atmosphere around the table was a friendly one. Deep in thought, Annalise ate her food which was thankfully tasty. She fondly remembered the warmth in Mr. Shaw's eyes when he first saw her on the platform. The way that he'd helped her up from the ground and how he'd defended her from Carter.

But a great burden fell heavy on her heart as she thought also of his hostility, his unwillingness to have her because of Jamie, and the way he didn't seem to respect God. She felt lost and alone, despite Jamie being seated right beside her. These woes were not ones that she could share with him. She would not tell him of the fear in her heart when she considered if she had made the right decision. A wave of homesickness washed over her. Not for the brothel and the horrid Madam. But for her deceased mother and her best friend Lucy. She quickly nodded her head to herself; she would write a letter to her friend that very night. That was the hope that she clung to for the rest of the evening.

Chapter Seven

Reid rode upon Lycan's back, the leather saddle shifting under his weight, his reins loose in his hands. Wade rode beside them on his own palomino, Racer. The white-legged, pastel yellow horse contrasted Lycan's blue-gray color. The sun was a little hot that day. It beat down on them, threatening to turn them into mush. Reid wiped away a bead of sweat that was about to drip into his eye. Thankfully, he and Wade had been able to maintain a good number of trees within the pastures which allowed the cattle to have access to plenty of shade.

They moved throughout the pastures, checking in on the cattle while Reid ranted and complained about Annalise in between each cattle check.

"I just don't understand why she has to say a blessing before every meal. If it was just dinner, that would be bearable, although still annoying. But I go to eat some grits first thing in the morning and I have to sit through her prayers. I really don't even think God cares if we say a blessing or not. It's more for her own satisfaction at making me have to wait before eating. And don't get me started on her Bible reading. She has that thing with her everywhere. How much time can a woman really spend with her Bible? I'm not sure that I can take much more of this." He let out a large sigh and his body drooped as he expressed his exasperation. Wade let out a chuckle.

Reid glared at him. "What's so funny?" The horses continued, dodging around trees and maneuvering around bushes and large rocks.

Wade shook his head, like he wasn't sure where to begin, "You put out a flyer for a mail-order bride. You could have received a woman with any number of flaws. The only one you see in Miss Owens is that she's too religious. Now is that really even a flaw at all? I know a lot of men who would celebrate that rather than be opposed to it."

"It is a flaw," Reid argued. "I wanted a bride to help me with things around the ranch. To make my life easier. Not to hinder and annoy me... And she has other flaws too," he insisted. Even to himself, he thought he sounded a little like a child throwing a temper tantrum.

They continued to ride as a silence fell over them, both men lost in thought. Reid quickly rolled his eyes at himself, with a wish that she would stop getting to him. Ever since he had brought her home, he couldn't seem to get her out of his mind. The spare bedroom has already been prepared for her before going to the station that day. Her bringing a child along wasn't in the plans, but it hadn't taken too much more effort to accommodate the young one. A few ranch hands had moved a second bed into the spare room, and he hadn't needed much else.

On the way home from the train station, Reid had worried about the boy, wondering what kind of problems he would cause. Would he terrorize the horses and cattle? Would he damage property or keep the men up all hours of the night? To Reid's surprise, however, the boy had been no trouble at all. He never saw him without Miss Owens, and the boy didn't seem to misbehave much. He minded his manners and always did as she asked. Reid wondered about the two of them while he rubbed his face absentmindedly. She claimed that he wasn't her child and that she had never been with a man. But without knowing any better, the pair truly looked like mother and child.

Not only did they both look very similar with dark hair and green eyes, but Miss Owens was incredibly caring and tender with the boy. Reid had often observed them when they didn't realize that he was watching. He had been outside once, mending a fence on the south side of the house when he heard people talking. He decided to allow himself a small break to see what was going on. After he stepped around the edge of the fence, he saw that Miss Owens and the boy were outside and in the process of hanging up clothing on the drying line.

In between articles of clothing, Miss Owens would chase the boy around before they would tumble into the grass in a fit of laughter and tickles. This continued numerous times until the clothes were all hung up, and then they headed back inside, the boy skipping through the grass while Miss Owens slowly followed. Reid had returned to his fence, but all afternoon the image of them playing in between chores had repeated in his mind causing him to smile more than he had in a long time.

Reid had also noticed that Miss Owens always allowed the boy to help with the preparation of meals. He found this to be pretty incredible, and a good indicator of Miss Owens' patience, as the boy often made messes or did the wrong thing. They had been in the process of making loaves of bread that morning while Reid was finishing his cup of coffee at the table. Miss Owens tasked the child with dumping cups of flour into the bowl. The first one he completed successfully but with the second cup, he began to tip it over much sooner than he should have which caused flour to fall everywhere, covering the counter and floor and dusting the air.

While Reid in the next room had been frustrated by the mistake, Miss Owens had been as calm and gentle as ever, showing the boy how to help clean it up and try again with a new cup of flour.

Throughout the day, she was constantly praising the boy, encouraging him, and showing him kindness and love. Reid knew that if she ever had children of her own, she would be a great mother to them as well. He wondered again about their future. He never said how long the trial would last, and Miss Owens never asked. While she hadn't been with them for very long yet, Reid could feel an internal pressure to make a decision. He wanted to stop agonizing over what he was going to do. The thought of kicking her out and sending her away made his heart hurt and his shoulders slump. But he wasn't sure that he could have her as his wife with the boy in the picture as a constant reminder of Miss Owens' ability to be deceitful.

"Hey, look up there," Wade said, calling Reid's attention back to the present. He blinked in surprise, uncertain of how long he had been lost in thought. He studied the area ahead of them and immediately noticed what Wade had been referring to. Up the hill, a cow was lying flat on its side and didn't seem to be moving. Something was definitely wrong. Reid nudged his heels into Lycan's side and they raced forward to the cow. As soon as they neared it, he pulled Lycan to a stop and jumped out of the saddle before he jogged the last of the way. Wade had galloped along with him and also dismounted. Instead of examining the cow though, he looked around, trying to ascertain any other facts concerning the situation.

Reid made a few clicking noises with his mouth in an attempt to not startle the cow. Her eye opened and watched him as he approached but then she closed her eyes, not even bothering to move or try and stand. Reid patted her neck. "What happened here, girl? What's going on?"

He touched along her and then studied her breathing for a moment. He could immediately tell that the animal's breathing was shallow. Her body trembled slightly and a small amount of sweat had started to cause her hide to glisten. All of the poor beast's energy was going into trying to survive. Reid gently felt along her side, making sure that nothing was broken or otherwise injured. Even as he searched, he found no wounds or injuries that would explain the odd behavior.

As Reid examined her, he noticed Wade moving out of the corner of his eye. He looked up to see that his friend had spotted another cow nearby. Wade headed towards it, walking slowly so as to not spook it. This cow was standing but just barely. Even from a distance, Reid could see that it was breathing shallowly and had tremors across its body as well just like the poor girl in front of him.

Fear seeped into his veins. He stood up and quickly called to his friend. "Something's very wrong. I'm going to get the vet." He hurried back over to Lycan and quickly mounted, pulling himself off the ground with his foot in the stirrup.

"This cow is ill as well. I'll wait here with them while you're gone," Wade confirmed. Reid nodded to him and then urged his horse back towards the ranch.

They raced across the pastures and dodged the features of the landscape. Some cattle that appeared to be healthy were stunned by Reid's sudden appearance and took off running across the grass. As he reached the edge of the pasture, he slowed Lycan down long enough to unlock the fence, get them out, and relock it before they were quickly headed down the road again. In order to get to the main path away from his ranch and towards the vet, he had to pass by the house.

He didn't think much about it until he spotted Miss Owens on the porch. She had been watering the flowers in their small pots that were dotted along the porch. She looked up in surprise at the sound of his horse's hooves pounding the dirt path. Seeing Reid, Miss Owens dropped her watering can, her hands fluttering up to her chest in surprise. A flood of emotions hits Reid when he sees the concern on Miss Owens' face. Without even thinking, he began to slow down Lycan and angled him to ride beside the porch.

"Some of the cattle are sick. I'm going to fetch the doctor," he explained quickly, still mostly out of breath from the ride.

"Oh, no," Miss Owens said. She seemed to be genuinely concerned. "I'll go pray for you and them immediately." With a quick nod of her head, she hurried back inside the ranch house. Reid could only assume she would go up to her room, drop to her knees at her bed, fold her hands together, and pray over his livestock.

He was slightly touched by her actions, recognizing that she seemed to be a very kind and compassionate person. But again with the praying? He gritted his teeth together and urged his horse forward once more, racing down the track to where the local veterinary doctor lived. His cattle farm was his whole life, and he was going to do everything in his power to make sure his cows didn't die.

Chapter Eight

At dinner the evening that the sick cattle were discovered, Annalise was disappointed to find that Mr. Shaw was not in attendance. Earlier she had noticed how upset and worried he was about the sick cattle but she wasn't sure what the outcome had been. Thankfully, once the men were settled at the table with their plates piled high with food, they talked about what had happened after Mr. Shaw brought back the veterinarian.

Apparently, the men had spent all afternoon gathering up the cows that were sick. They had herded the animals to a specific barn to keep them separate from the rest of the herd. Annalise learned that this was for the safety of the healthy cows as well as for the benefit of the sick cows so that the doctor and Mr. Shaw could keep a closer eye on them. Before going to bed that night, Annalise repeated her prayer that had echoed throughout her mind the entire day, hoping that the cattle would be alright.

The next morning's breakfast passed in a rush. She found that she was happy to see Mr. Shaw as he came to get a plate, although he was already gone by the time Annalise and Jamie had come to the table to sit down. All the other farm hands left quickly as well. With a lonely pain in her chest, Annalise started the long process of cleaning up all the dishes and taking care of the extra food. Jamie never focused very long when it came to cleaning up, so she had sent him away to play while she worked.

"Look Annalise," Jamie said, his youthful voice easily breaking past her thoughts. She turned to see that he had a large cowboy hat on his head. Mr. Shaw's hat, to be specific.

Annalise gasped and quickly stepped away from the sink which was full of warm water, bubbles, and dirty plates.

"Where did you get this from?" she asked. She quickly dried her hands on her apron and walked over to take the hat off of Jamie's head. The boy turned and headed to the dining room to show her where he had found it. He quickly pointed out Mr. Shaw's chair.

"It was just sitting there. Can I play with it again?" he asked, a hint of begging in his voice.

"No," Annalise answered. "This is Mr. Shaw's hat. It's not something you're able to play with." Jamie frowned but didn't argue further. He got some jacks and marbles from his pocket and quickly set them up on the floor to play with instead.

Annalise headed back to the kitchen and placed the hat carefully on a higher shelf so that Jamie couldn't reach it again. She went back to the dishes while her thoughts were swirling around her mind. Mr. Shaw was never without his hat. He must have been so focused on getting back out to the sick cattle that he forgot about it. Even so, she knew that he would be missing it. She glanced up at the worn item. It seemed like the hat had seen many years of wear, with crinkle lines in the leather and dirt caked into parts of it.

The stitching seemed to be worn out and Annalise wondered how much use it had left in it. A small part of her wanted to make or purchase a new one for him, but she quickly shook the silly notion way. He wouldn't accept a gift from her. Besides, she had no money that would enable her to do so.

She finished the dishes and had them all set out on a towel to dry, and then went to find Jamie. "Would you like to go read some of your picture books up in our room? I need to return Mr. Shaw's hat to him. I won't be long."

"I guess," he said, "but I don't want to clean this up." He gestured to his marbles and jacks that were spread out across the floor.

"I'll help you," Annalise told him. She quickly lowered to the floor and swept the pieces into her hand. Once they were done, she walked Jamie up to their room. As they walked up the stairs, Annalise looked the framed pictures that adorned the walls. Most of them were painted family portraits or still lives of vases with flowers. None of them seemed very newly created and she assumed that Mr. Shaw's mother, or some other woman, had made them based on the illegible, sprawling scripted name that signed the bottom of all of them.

They reached the second floor of the large ranch house where light poured into the hallway from the open doors of three of the bedrooms. Two of the rooms, which Annalise had just cleaned a few days prior at Mr. Shaw's request, were unoccupied quaint rooms. They were well furnished with a bed, wardrobe, table and curtains drawn back from the windows, but they were missing residents; like new shoes waiting for an owner. One of the unoccupied rooms seemed to be more feminine in style and color, and Annalise had wondered briefly who had lived in it before.

A fourth door stood at the end of the hallway was closed off, the darkest point in the hallway. Mr. Shaw was very private over his own room, and never left the door open. The third open door was to the room that she shared with Jamie. It was similar to the two unoccupied rooms but with two beds now instead of one. Their small amount of clothing fit easily into the wardrobe that was provided, leaving a large portion of it empty. She doubted that they would ever be able to fill the entire thing, but she hoped that someday, they would have more garments than they do now.

One of her favorite things about their room was the view. Their window looked out along the back side of the property where many acres filled with cattle and horses were spread out. At the first light the morning, when she got up to pray before she woke Jamie for the day, she would look outside at God's beautiful masterpiece. She was always so amazed that she got to live somewhere with so much beauty.

In their room, Annalise helped Jamie set up some of his books and toys in the open space on the rug. She was soon satisfied that Jamie would be able to keep himself entertained while she stepped out. She quickly slid on her boots and headed downstairs and out the front door.

The bright sun immediately fell across her face, feeling good in contrast to the fall breeze that had started recently. She knew then that bringing the hat out to Mr. Shaw was a good choice, as she didn't want him to get a sunburn. She headed towards the barn she had seen Mr. Shaw and Mr. Barnes go into the most within the last day. It must be where they were keeping the sick cattle. As she walked, one of the farm dogs ran up to her, tail wagged excessively, tongue hung lazily from its mouth as it almost seemed to smile at her. She stopped to quickly pet the black scruffy herding dog. Since arriving at the ranch, Annalise had quickly made friends with all the farm dogs as she had always been friendly with the stray dogs who wandered the neighborhood that the brothel was in.

This dog in particular had seemed to take quite a liking to her. When no one was watching, Annalise gave the sweet animal lots of pats and scratches around its ears. It was not often that she saw the ranch hands stop what they were doing to pet the dogs, and she often wondered if she would get into trouble for doing so. The men seemed to appreciate the dogs on the ranch even though they didn't show them much affection. It seemed that they treated the dogs more like working animals than pets. Despite this, every day when Annalise fed them she always made sure that the dogs shared the leftover food that she would give out to them on the back porch. She wanted to make sure that they were all treated fairly.

While Annalise was immediately comfortable around the dogs from the first day that she arrived on the ranch, it was the cows and bulls that made her the most anxious. They were much larger than any animal in the city, other than horses, and she figured it would take her a lot longer to get used to and feel comfortable around the cattle, especially if she spent all her time away from them.

The dog zipped around her feet and raced along as it followed her across the lawn and to the quarantine barn. From what Annalise had seen of the property, the barn that Mr. Shaw was putting the sick cattle into was one of the more medium-sized ones, painted a dull gray color with a brown roof. It was nestled in between some other barns and equipment sheds of similar colors. Annalise understood why Mr. Shaw had chosen this barn. It was near the house, so he could get to it quickly day or night, and it was a good distance from all the other places where animals were often kept, like the main grazing pastures. Annalise reached the barn door, and with the hat in hand, she pulled the door open. The farm dog immediately shot into the barn. Annalise started to follow it when a commotion erupted ahead of her inside of the barn. Lots of cows began to low in a nervous and worried tone, their cries soon turned into a chorus.

"Hey, get out of here!"

"Go on, get!" cried two different voices. Annalise recognized them as Mr. Shaw and Mr. Barnes. Their yelling helped her understand her mistake. She had let the dog into the barn and it had startled the sick cattle.

She began to whistle for the dog. "Come here, boy," she called. It soon raced past her and back outside the barn. Annalise stepped outside with it and immediately worked on trying to pull the door shut right after herself, with the hope that the dog wouldn't be able to get back inside the barn. Suddenly a hand grabbed the edge of the door and forced it back open. Mr. Shaw stepped through and then pull the door closed behind him. As soon as their eyes met, Annalise knew that she was in a heap of trouble.

"What are you doing out here? Why are you interfering with my business?" Mr. Shaw asked, his face getting heated. His jaw was clenched tight between each word.

"I'm so sorry," Annalise began to stutter as she took a step backward. Her heart jumped in her chest with apprehension.

"Those cattle are sick," he continued with a disappointed frown as he squinted at her. "And you just let the dog in there to terrorize them while they are feeling so vulnerable and poorly."

"I didn't mean to," Annalise tried to explain. "He slipped in as soon as I had the door wide enough..." Her hands shook and she racked her brain, trying to come up with an explanation that Mr. Shaw might accept.

But Mr. Shaw only shook his head in a slow and tired way. "I don't think this is working out," he said. A small gasp escaped Annalise as he spoke. "I just can't help but feel like you would be much better off back in the city. I don't think the country is for you."

"Please…don't send me back. I will work harder, I promise," Annalise said, her voice cracking and her hands shaking with shock. She felt like her throat was closing and she tilted her head slightly up in an attempt to keep the tears from coming.

Mr. Shaw said nothing and seemed to refuse to even look at her, not wanting to meet her gaze. Annalise attempted to calm her breathing but wasn't having much success. She handed him his hat, which was still in her hand, back to him.

He looked at the hat with wide surprise, having not noticed it previously in her hands. He took it from her with a softness in his eyes that Annalise hadn't noticed before. But rather than wait for him to say something, and not wanting him to see her cry, she quickly turned and ran away from the barn, her dress swishing against her as she moved. She raced back to the house, not bothering to slow down or glance behind her as the tears streamed down her face.

Chapter Nine

That evening, the night air was chilly and the crickets sang loudly in time with the fireflies that danced around the sky. Reid tapped his finger on the glass cup in his hand, deep in thought. Wade sat beside him on the front porch. They rocked in wooden rocking chairs as they drank in general silence. The only light came from the stars and full moon, which lit up the ground and allowed the men to see their surroundings with little difficulty.

There had been many times since meeting Wade that they would sit and rock on the porch, although it was not a nightly routine. It had become somewhat of a safe space for Reid. The days were filled with endless tasks of taking care of the ranch, animals, and men. When the sun finally decided to go down, it always seemed to Reid that it was giving him permission to have some time to himself too. Although there were candles, lanterns, and fires, none of them ever did such a good job of lighting things up.

It was difficult to work in the dark. So, when the light finally ceased in the sky, all the creatures would settle and get ready for sleep. But sleep never came easily for him. Polly had always been able to fall asleep with ease and not too many noises could rouse her. Since his parents had died though, Reid always had a small part of himself that thought he should always be awake, ready for any trouble that might come. There were many years where he would only fall asleep from pure exhaustion, and even then he would wake up within a few hours, restless and unable to drift off again.

The solution to his sleeping problem came in the form of sitting in the rocking chair and relaxing. When they had first started working together, Wade had noticed that Reid didn't like to sleep, or rather, had a hard time falling and staying asleep. He had found him on the porch late one night. Reid had been sitting on the edge of it, letting his legs dangle while he rubbed his face and uttered frustrated words. By himself, sitting on the porch had felt like he was failing at sleep. Like he was unable to do what other people and creatures did with ease. But when Wade was with him, it no longer seemed like a problem, and more like a solution. Reid had found that just a few hours of porch time, sitting and relaxing after the long day had helped him far more than tossing and turning in his bed for hours on end.

That night in particular, it was far past their bedtime, and all the other ranch hands were already asleep in their building on the other side of the ranch. Although Reid had often offered for Wade to stay with him at the ranch house, Wade always declined, saying that he should bunk with the workers. While Wade never stayed in the ranch house, there were quite a few times in the past years when Reid would stay with the ranch hands, only returning to the ranch house to prepare meals for his men. Since Miss Owens' arrival, he had always stayed in the ranch house. It was important to him that he was nearby and easy to reach in case she ever needed anything. It was her first time out in the country after all.

Tonight, Reid had returned to the ranch house after the evening chores. Unable to even think about sleeping, he headed to the porch with a drink in hand. Wade had appeared within the hour, gotten his own drink, and sat down to join Reid. Somehow, Wade always seemed to know when he couldn't sleep. While they sat in a comfortable silence, it was one filled with unspoken words, but Reid wasn't fully sure if he even knew what words needed to be said, let alone have the ability to say them.

Reid thought back over the last two days since they had found the sick cattle and he had brought Dr. Harris back to the ranch. The vet had looked carefully over the sick animals. He listened to their hearts and lungs, checked their ears, eyes, and mouths, and gave the rest of their bodies a general inspection.

"These cows must have eaten something that they shouldn't have," Harris had said. "The lethargy, the tremors… I've seen this before." He had shaken his head.

"Is there something we can do? Something that we can give them?" Reid had asked, not allowing himself to hope.

The doctor had shaken his head again. "Unfortunately not. We just have to wait and see if they survive." Reid's heart had sunk low in his chest. "What you've done here with the barn is great. Just keep them comfortable and away from any stressors. They will overeat, so don't give them too much feed, but make sure they have water at all times. It's going to be a tough night for them."

"Is there any possibility that it could spread to the rest of the cattle?"

Dr. Harris had pursed his lips together. "As long as none of the other cattle eat what made these ones sick, they should be just fine." He'd patted Reid's shoulder before moving to clean up his medical equipment. It was a long ride back to his property and he had to be prepared for the next patient in need.

Reid had spent the rest of the day working hard to keep the cows comfortable, and then Miss Owens had let the dog in. He let out a sigh of exhaustion.

"You've always been so meticulous about the fields," Wade spoke suddenly. His words broke Reid from his thoughts.

"I sure try," he replied and took a sip of his drink.

"More than try," Wade insisted. "You're always having the men check through the fields and getting rid of any plants that could do the cattle harm. For years I haven't seen a harmful plant grow past an inch before you got it out of the ground and into the bonfire."

"I guess I'm going to have to work even harder in the future."

Wade shook his head, and his mouth twisted up. "I don't think this was caused by some plants growing in the fields. I think this was caused by a person looking for trouble." Reid cocked his head to the side, considering. It wasn't a farfetched idea, unfortunately. Wade continued, growing confident, "Your ranch is the most successful in the area. If a competitor wanted to cause you some harm, it would be relatively simple the sneak onto the outskirts of the land some drop something poisonous for the cattle to find."

"That's not something that we can prove, unfortunately," Reid said. His free hand clenched into a fist. "I have good relations with all the surrounding ranches, except one. The same one that's just a bit larger and more successful than mine."

"Carter's," Wade said, with a knowing shake of his head.

Reid ground his teeth together. "If I find out that that fool did something to my cattle to put them in danger, all because he feels threatened by me... Even you won't be able to hold me back." He gave his friend a knowing look. Then he leaned back in his chair, trying to let go of the fiery anger that was holding his heart. Until he had proof that his cattle had been wronged, he would have to control himself. The two men fell back into silence but this time, Reid's leg bounced up and down as his thoughts remained uneasy, but he wasn't thinking about Carter.

"What's on your mind?" Wade asked. The benefit, and sometimes drawback, of being so close to his foreman for so long was that he could always tell when something was wrong.

Reid let out a heavy sigh. "I was so harsh with her today... after she let the dog into the barn." Wade gave a knowing nod. Although the doors of the barn were thick, he had heard what Reid had told Miss Owens. "And I feel really bad for upsetting her," Reid continued. "But she seems to be so out of place here on the farm. And I just can't help but wonder if she would be better off someplace else."

He ran a hand through his hair, his conflicting emotions eating at him. Since bringing her to the ranch, he had watched not only how she was with the boy, but how she handled the country life as well. Her first few days, she was so wide-eyed. The cattle seemed to frighten her, and she didn't look very comfortable around the horses. He knew that she would have no idea what to do if he handed her a hammer or asked her to move the cattle to a different pasture.

He did silently admit to himself that her cooking had improved from the first night. She always had everything ready before the men arrived and he appreciated not having to do all the cooking and cleaning himself. Since Miss Owens had arrived, he'd been able to focus more on the ranch animals and his workers now that he didn't have to worry about the domestic side of things.

Just as he'd guessed, having a woman in the house had made his life generally easier with fewer tasks to worry about each day. But he hated how uncomfortable and out of place she seemed to be. She had agreed to be with him to get out of a life that she didn't want, and he couldn't help but wonder if she had accidentally fallen into a different version of an uncomfortable reality she couldn't escape.

A cry startled him from his thoughts, and he immediately bolted up from his chair which rocked into the back of his legs due to his quick departure. He and Wade both listened and could tell that the sound was coming from above them in the second story of the house. Reid nodded to his friend and then quickly headed inside. He placed his drink down on the first surface that he came to before he climbed up the stairs, taking them two at a time.

The light in Miss Owens' room was on and it shone through the bottom of the door. As he stepped closer, he could see that the door was just slightly open. He leaned forward to peek through the gap. He could see that Miss Owens, dressed in her nightgown, was on the child's bed. She was comforting him with back rubs and whispered words. Reid turned to leave, knowing she had it taken care of. But then she looked up, as if sensing his presence, and her green eyes found him as he looked through the crack of the door.

Chapter Ten

Jamie had woken up crying profusely from a nightmare. The sudden sounds had startled Annalise awake and she hurried over to his bed and in a rush to comfort him. She took him into her arms and cuddled him until he stopped crying. This was his first nightmare since arriving at the ranch. But Annalise remembered that, for weeks after their mother died, Jamie would cry through the night, unable to rest peacefully. For some reason, something about traveling and moving on from the brothel had soothed Jamie and for the first time in a while, he had fallen asleep with little issue and sleep throughout the night. But tonight was different.

Once he had settled down a bit, she took him out of her lap and placed him beside her on the bed, rubbing his back in soothing circles. "Are you alright?" she asked. He sniffled, still not seeming himself. "Did you have a bad dream?" Annalise continued, trying to understand.

Finally, he spoke in a shaky voice, "Mom was there, and she was taking care of us, but then she disappeared. And I couldn't find her." He turned to look at Annalise. "And you wouldn't help me look for her." Tears welled up in the corners of his eyes.

"Shh, shh," Annalise whispered to him while holding him close. "I'm so sorry that that happened in your dream." Her heart ached for her poor baby brother who had lost his mother far too soon. She had been fortunate to grow up with their mother, and he would never have that luxury. A calmer silence fell over them as Jamie settled down and Annalise started to wonder how she was going to get him to fall back asleep. Then she heard a noise from outside the room. She turned to look at the door and could just see, through the crack between the door and frame, that Mr. Shaw was watching them.

Her breath hitched in surprise and a wave of fear crashed inside of her. Jamie must have been too loud and woken Mr. Shaw. He was going to come yell at her again and remind her that she wouldn't be staying here much longer. Unease dug its way into her heart but she continued to look at Mr. Shaw, uncertain as to how she should proceed. But then, a small, kind smile took over his face and sympathy seemed to leak out of him. She blinked in surprise and wondered if he was a hallucination of her tired mind. But then he pushed the door open further, his sweet smile still in place.

Annalise feels a rush of heat flood her cheeks and crawl up her neck. For a moment, she wished that she could sink into the floor, and yet, she wasn't sure why. Mr. Shaw stepped into the room and it was like he was an entirely different person from the one she knew of during the day. Gone was the anger and temper that flared up so regularly. In its place was a kind, gentle, and calm man who appeared to be checking on them.

"Are you alright?" he asked Jamie. He waited for a response with his full attention fixed on Jamie as if he really cared about the answer.

"Yes, thank you," Annalise answered for her brother. "Jamie is okay."

"It sounded like you were pretty upset, Jamie," Mr. Shaw said. He squatted down slightly, getting closer to their level on the bed.

Jamie turned to look at Mr. Shaw with a sniff as he stuck out his lip. "I had a bad dream."

"Mmm." Mr. Shaw nodded in understanding as if bad dreams were something that he regularly experienced. The man looked thoughtful for a moment before his face brightened slightly. "Would you like a story to help you fall back asleep?" Annalise froze in surprise. Never in a million years would she have expected Mr. Shaw to tell a bedtime story.

Jamie, however, wasn't shocked by the offer and a small smile crept onto his face before turning so wide that all of his teeth could be seen. "Yes, sir."

"Okay," Mr. Shaw said. He seemed to be excited as there was extra energy in his step as he turned to grab the empty chair from the corner of the room. He pulled it over to the bed and quickly settled into it. His mouth was pursed as he considered what tale to tell the young boy. Annalise shifted Jamie so that he was lying down in bed once more, all tucked in, and cuddled up to her side.

"Are you all ready?" Mr. Shaw asked with some excitement in his voice. Jamie nodded again with another toothy smile. "Once upon a time," Mr. Shaw began, "there was a boy. He was older than you, but he still had lots of years of growing to do and it would be a while before he could be considered a grown-up." Jame nodded in understanding. "Well, this boy lived with his two parents and baby sister on a cattle ranch."

"Like this one?" Jamie interrupted.

"Much like this one," Mr. Shaw answered. He didn't seem to be fazed by the interruption, which Annalise appreciated. "They had many acres of pastures that were filled with all kinds of cattle and horses. The boy's life seemed to be perfect, but then one day everything changed. He lost his parents."

Annalise's body tensed at Mr. Shaw's words. She glanced down at Jamie with worry.

Jamie's forehead was covered with crease lines. "Did his sister help look for them?"

Mr. Shaw sighed sadly. "They both looked long and hard, but finally after many days of searching, they had to accept that their parents wouldn't be coming back."

"It was the Lord's plan," Jamie interrupted with a knowing shake of his head. Inside Annalise's heart, she had a small battle between being proud of his take on the character's parents dying and also being sad that Jamie already knew what it felt like to be like this orphaned character. The arm that she had wrapped around Jamie drew him in closer, wanting to soothe the poor boy.

Mr. Shaw frowned but continued telling the story, only slightly deterred. "And even though the young boy still had many years of growing to do, he took these life events as a challenge. He wanted to show the world that he could rise above his hardships and misfortune and still become successful. So, he started to work very hard, every day. He took care of the cattle and horses and did his best to learn all that he could.

And as he got older, he was able to expand the ranch more and more, until it was gigantic. Everyone in all the neighboring towns knew of his ranch. Many people came to him for jobs or resources, wanting to be a part of his prosperity." Annalise felt Jamie's body grow limp beside her and she knew he had fallen asleep. Mr. Shaw hadn't seemed to notice and continued telling his story. She sat quietly and allowed him to keep talking.

Part of her felt bad for not saying anything. Most likely, Mr. Shaw would rather be asleep right now. But the other part of her was enjoying this. Every other time that Mr. Shaw was around he was grumpy or focused on his work. This was the first time that Annalise could think of when he actually seemed to be enjoying himself in her vicinity.

Mr. Shaw continued his story, "However, there were a few others who couldn't seem to be happy for him. They did their best to take his focus off of all the blessings in his life and instead noticed all the flaws. Thankfully for the boy, he had his sister and his community to help him. But most of all, he also had himself to rely upon. And he knew that as long as he worked hard enough, he would succeed."

At the beginning of the story, Annalise had only noticed all the similarities that it had to Jamie. Dead parent, only a sister for company. But that's where the similarities ended. If Annalise had been telling the story, she would have fashioned it around Jamie. However, the more she thought about it, the more she realized that the main character had probably been fashioned around someone he knew. Someone like himself.

Annalise felt her heart drop with the understanding that Mr. Shaw had told them a story from his own life. The storytelling trailed off as Mr. Shaw looked up and saw that Jamie was fast asleep. They made eye contact and Annalise's thoughts swirled wildly and she wondered if she should acknowledge that she understood who the story was about. Instead, she decided to smile gently at him for the kind service that he had provided to Jamie. "Thank you, Mr. Shaw," she said. "He never falls asleep so easily during my stories."

"Reid," he said. "You can call me Reid. And thank you for listening, Miss Owens."

"Annalise," she told him with a smile.

"Annalise," he whispered quietly. He said her name for the first time like he was tasting it.

She felt lulled into his voice as he said her name and she was reminded of the way he spoke during the story, the way that his voice calmed her. All at once she had a feeling like a moth being drawn to a flame and she wished that she was closer to him. Their eyes locked, and Annalise marveled at the wonderful golden color of his eyes.

Then, all of a sudden, the spell was broken. Mr. Shaw-- or Reid, she corrected herself, stood up sharply, and just as quick as he had arrived, he was gone. The door clicked shut behind him.

Annalise blinked in surprise but with his absence, it was as if the air had been returned to the room. She rubbed her face with her hands and wondered what was happening to her. She had never felt this way before, as if her world could be so drastically changed by the presence of a person or by their absence. The way he had acted tonight had been so different from every other time they had interacted. It was as if, during the peace of the night, he had been peaceful as well. She slipped out of Jamie's bed, put out her candle, and then crawled into her own while her thoughts continued.

The last time Reid had mentioned her leaving had been at the barn that day. It hadn't been brought up again and she wondered if he didn't intend to follow through with what he had said. When they argued, she felt as if she would be happier leaving this place. But in moments like before, there was a small hope in her chest. She wanted to stay and see if she could become friends, maybe even partners in marriage, with the peaceful man of the night.

Chapter Eleven

Carter Johnson sat upon his piebald horse. The horse's reins were pulled into a tight bunch in his hands which caused the horse to shift its mouth uncomfortably. It stomped its feet on the ground occasionally, attempting to keep the flies from landing on it.

Atop his horse, Carter watched the acres ahead of him curiously, his brown, narrow eyes searched anxiously for any sign that something was amiss. He sat on his horse just on the edge of the property line to the Shaw ranch. For the past week, he had made numerous trips to town and did his best to linger in the saloons and general stores.

These trips had been made with the purpose of gathering all the town's gossip. To his great disappointment, however, not once did anyone say anything about sick cows on Shaw's land. Instead, there was plenty of talk about the Hatfield affair and old man Harty who had died by falling in a well. At one point he had heard two women whispering about the lady that Shaw had picked up at the train station, but they mostly seemed disappointed that he was likely not going to be a bachelor much longer. Not once did they mention his herd getting sick or even better, dying.

Part of Carter wanted to go interrogate the vet, but he knew that if no one else was talking about this misfortune on Shaw's ranch, then he would give himself away if he brought it up. Besides, he needed the vet for his own cattle. That was one man who Carter made an effort to be friendly with. So, when his trips to town were unsuccessful, he had taken to patrolling the border, looking for signs that his plan was working.

But even when he returned to the site where he had left the poison, he was hard-pressed to find a sick cow. It had taken a few nights of heavy drinking before the solution had come to him. The girl. That city girl who Shaw had picked up at the train station. She was the answer. Upon realizing this, Carter slammed down his glass on the table in victory. It wouldn't take much charm to get the girl to tell him what he needed to know. All he needed was to get her alone, make her feel safe, and get her to start talking.

So now he sat on his horse at the border of Shaw's ranch. He figured that the trickiest part of his plan would be finding the girl without running into Shaw, but he was up for the challenge. He kicked his heels roughly into his horse's side, and they headed into Reid Shaw's territory. While he normally enjoyed riding his horse as fast, and faster, than it was willing to run, today he took it easy. He knew that patience would be very important so that he wasn't caught red-handed on his enemy's ranch before he got information. He didn't mind being found on the ranch after talking to the girl, but he needed to get information prior to being caught.

As he rode, he glared at his surroundings. In his mind, he compared not only the cattle that he could see but also the dirt, the grass, the other crops, and even the streams to his own. He smiled to himself, knowing his own land to be superior, even though the geographical qualities of the two properties were nearly identical, other than his being larger of course. When he started to see the barns and ranch house up ahead, he watched them carefully, checking to see if he should change his route or maybe hide somewhere. To his excitement though, the only men that he saw were headed out on their horses toward a pasture in the opposite direction as him. He was free and clear to head to the house.

He urged his horse into a faster gait and soon he was at the house. He found a hitching post easily and quickly tied up his horse. Before approaching the door, he took a moment to smooth back his hair and dust off any dirt that had gathered along his shirt and pants. He had to look fresh to maintain his reputation of course. Then he approached the door and gave it a couple of solid taps on the wood. When someone didn't immediately answer the door, he began to knock harder and longer, his impatience already bleeding through and into his actions.

Just as he was about to start knocking again, the girl answered the door. "Hello, can I help you?" she asked.

"Hello my dear, I'm Carter Johnson," he said with a great big smile, the largest he could muster. "I was looking for Reid, I'm a very close friend of his; who might you be?"

"Oh, I'm Annalise Owens… weren't you at the train station?" she asked, looking at him suspiciously.

"Oh yes, of course, that's right. Reid was there picking you up. I'm so happy to see that you've settled in alright." He smiled largely at her, but she didn't return the same expression.

She pointed out towards one of the back pastures that Carter had seen mounted men heading to. "I believe you can find Reid out in that direction." She stepped back farther from the door, looking like she was about to close it.

"Oh, but my dear Annalise, I have journeyed a long way and I don't think I have the energy to go find Reid out there. I know your land is incredibly vast." He smiled again while he wiped at his face. "Besides, it's rude to turn away a friend in this town."

The girl looked thoughtful. "Would you like to come in and sit down? I have some coffee brewing if you would like any. Although I'm not sure when Reid will be back to the house. He's normally out working all day, although some of the hands will be coming in soon for their afternoon break."

"That would be wonderful," he said quickly before pushing through the door past her. "Although," he said, rubbing at his beard, "Coffee upsets my stomach. Some fresh tea would be perfect." Annalise frowned but led him to the dining room. She gestured for him to sit before she headed into the kitchen to begin making a fresh pot of tea. "So how has your time at the ranch been so far? Has anything exciting happened?" he inquired.

"It's certainly different from the city," she said from the other room. "I'm enjoying how quiet it is out here. The sunsets are lovely, and the air always seems so fresh." She finished preparing the tea and brought a cup over for Carter. She stood awkwardly for a moment, unsure of what to do next. He gestured for her to sit at the table and so she did, but only on the edge of her chair.

"And your sick cows, how are they doing?" he asked as if everyone in town knew about them.

Annalise blinked in surprise before shaking her head with a smile. "They are doing much better and have recovered. The doctor said that Reid had found them at a good time, although all they really needed was some rest, food, and water to get better. Reid was very relieved when they all pulled through the night."

"What ended up making them so sick?" Carter asked with a frown.

"Reid said that there was some sort of flowering plant that was all over the edge part of the pasture. It was one he didn't recognize, and he and the workers immediately took care of it, pulling it out by the roots and burning it in a large bonfire outside of the pasture."

"I see," Carter said, unable to keep the disappointment out of his voice.

Annalise narrowed her eyes at him and stood up from her seat. "Reid did a great job taking care of the cattle and making sure that they wouldn't get sick again." There was pride in her voice while she spoke about Reid, and now she was looking suspiciously at him.

He carefully fixed his facial features into those of pleasantness once more. "I'm so glad that he was able to help the cattle. Having harm come to your herd is just about the worst feeling that a rancher can experience." Annalise nodded, seeming to be at ease with him once more. "This is some lovely tea," he said, though he'd barely touched the cup. Slowly he stood up from his chair, having discovered all he wanted to know. "There will always be a job open at my ranch if you are ever interested." He smiled at her, despite her frown.

A large bang sounded throughout the house as the front door slammed open. Annalise jumped at the sound, her hand darting to grab hold of the table to steady herself. The unexpected sound only caused his eye to twitch as he already knew who was storming in before Reid could even round the corner.

Chapter Twelve

Reid had been out with the ranch hands, checking on their herd to make sure that no other cattle had gotten sick when Peter, who had only been hired on at the beginning of the summer, had quickly rode up behind the group after a late start that morning. His horse stopped alongside the group without any issue but Peter himself was out of breath. "Did you get lost?" Wade joked and all the men shared a good laugh. Peter's cheeks darkened slightly and he ducked his face, embarrassed even though the jokes were not meant to be taken seriously.

"Just got stuck at the outhouse for a bit," the young hire explained unnecessarily. Before the men could protest at the direction the conversation was heading, Peter quickly changed topics, "Say, did any of you see that piebald that was hitched by the house? He sure was a beauty." Reid's head jerked at this and he turned Lycan to get a better view of the house which was a good deal behind them. He squinted, but couldn't make out any other details. His pulse raced as worry gnawed at his stomach. Annalise was at the house with an unknown visitor. Only one person reliably came to mind when he thought of a piebald horse.

He turned and his gaze met Wade. "Are you good here?"

Wade tilted his head slightly but nodded, "We're good, boss." Reid turned, clicked his tongue, and pressed his heels into Lycan's sides, nudging him to race back towards the ranch house. The trip back through the pastures was short as Lycan's long legs ate up the distance without even breaking a sweat. Reid reached the hitching post easily and saw that the piebald was indeed the one he knew to be Carter Johnson's horse.

Reid left Lycan a short distance away from his rival's horse and sprinted the rest of the way to the house. He reached the door and flung it open, not caring that it bounced off the inner wall at his arrival. He strode through the house in quick steps until he reached the dining room where he saw Carter sitting comfortably at the table, a teacup in his hands, and Annalise in the chair beside him.

"It's time for you to go," Reid said between clenched teeth, his hands balled up in fists. His body shook slightly at the effort of holding himself back. In his mind he imagined himself yelling the words at Carter. Or perhaps wrapping his hands around the man's throat. Both of the thoughts appeased him slightly, but not enough to cool the fire in his words and heart.

As if he owned the place, Carter stood up slowly, lazily placed the cup down on the table, and dusted off the front of his pants. "I'm *so* happy to hear that your cattle have recovered, Reid."

The words hit Reid like an icicle to the heart. Other than the people who lived on his land, only the doctor knew that he had sick animals. He always went to great lengths to keep his business private. None of his men would have dared to say a word or risk their good-paying jobs here. Yet Carter knew. Reid turned to look at Annalise as realization dawned on him. She had stood up from her chair and was facing him as her hands clenched and unclenched, fiddling with the front of her dress. Her gaze met his and she tilted her chin up with confidence even as her eyes dropped away from him.

A wave of anger crashed into Reid at both the thought of Annalise telling Carter private information and at him being there in the first place. He turned to the unwelcome guest. "Get off my land, Carter. You're not welcome here." Carter nodded his head and cooly took his leave. He headed through the house and out the door with a strong lack of urgency. The moment Reid heard him leave the house, his heavy steps echoing off the porch, he turned toward Annalise. His voice wavered but he did his best to keep it low and level, "Never let Carter into this house again." His eyes narrowed at her.

"I was just being neighborly," Annalise replied without any form of apology, although there was a hint of guilt in her words.

"That man is no neighbor," Reid said, his finger pointed aggressively toward where Carter had left. "He is nothing but a heap of trouble."

"How am I supposed to know that when you never tell me anything?" Annalise asked while throwing up her hands. She turned to him, her eyes wide and questioning as if she actually wanted an answer.

Reid's nostrils flared as he realized that Annalise was not going to accept the blame for this. He opened his mouth to respond but was unable to stay anything as the words jumped around in his mind. He could see the confusion and hurt on her face and he knew that he should explain himself. He tried to speak several times but when only grunts came out, he lifted his hat, pushed his hand through his hair, replaced his hat, and turned quickly to stomp back out of the house away from her. He knew that she was upset about him leaving, but it was better that he left now instead of saying something that he would regret. For when he was mad, his words sliced deeper than a freshly sharpened knife.

Chapter Thirteen

Annalise spent extra time that afternoon on the meal for the men. She figured that the best way to help resolve the dispute between Reid and herself was through a nice meal and hopefully, he would come to see that she hadn't intended to cause problems by sharing information with Carter. She dumped a few helpings of beans into the large pan and added some salted beef with it. It cooked for a while until all of it was bubbling. Once it was hot enough, she turned off the heat, put the lid on, and allowed it to simmer.

"Jamie, are you ready to go?" she called to him. He quickly appeared in the kitchen. As he walked, he attempted to stuff his toy soldiers in his pockets. Annalise washed her hands and gathered some woven baskets while he finished. Ready to go, they headed outside and to the back orchard where there were a few apple trees, among a variety of others.

The orchard was just a short walk away and although the day was nearly over, the sky was still bright and everyone was still hard at work. Annalise was happy that the heat from the day had started to fade and the wind provided a nice breeze. As they reached the trees, Annalise noticed that some of the riper apples had fallen onto the ground. "Take a look at those ones and see if any of them are still good. As long as they haven't gone rotten, we should be able to use them." Jamie excitedly started to examine the apples, his basket quickly filling up.

While Jamie worked on the apples on the ground, Annalise closely eyed the ones in the trees. She began to pluck the ones that looked ready to fall and gathered them in her own basket. "Do you see all these marks?" she asked Jamie, pointing out browned spots and indents that were on the sides of most of the apples.

"Yes, what are they from?" he asked.

"Those are spots where creatures have snacked on the apples. Sometimes bugs, sometimes birds. The apples on the ground might have been nibbled on by rabbits, chipmunks, and more."

"It looks like they've all been eaten," he said with a sigh.

"That's not a bad thing," she replied with a laugh. "These apples help feed us and God's other creatures. If we can share them, it's better for everyone. If the apple has been almost fully eaten, you can leave it, but if it only has a spot taken from a caterpillar, then we can still use it for our own food." She continued collecting apples to add to her basket. "Oh look here, this bug is eating right now." Jamie approached her and she lifted him up in the air to take a better look at the apple which had a long bug sticking out of it.

"Let's not pick that one," he said, not finding the same amusement.

After just a few minutes, they had plenty of apples to work with, even though there were still many that would need to be used within the next few days. "Is this good?" Jamie asked, his voice lit with enthusiasm as he showed her his nearly full basket.

"That's great," she told him with a smile as she ruffled his hair. With their baskets much heavier, they headed back to the house. Just outside, they stopped at the water well and pulled up some water to rinse off the apples, doing their best to keep all the bugs, leaves, and twigs outside the house. Then they carried the apples inside and set them down in the kitchen, happy to no longer be hauling the heavy load.

"What are you going to make with them?" Jamie asked, with a lick of his lips.

Annalise chuckled and gestured for him to take one. "I'm going to make some fried apples. I think it will be a nice treat after a hard day of work." Jamie grabbed his favorite apple from the bunch and quickly began to munch on it, his teeth breaking through the crispy skin with a crunch.

She gathered a few apples onto her cutting board and began to chop them up. Her knife was swift as it sliced, separating the good pieces from the core and bug-eaten spots. After making a large pile of chopped apples, she got the skillet ready and started heating some lard in it. Once it was sizzling, she began to add the apple pieces, allowing them to cook in the oil. Jamie watched the process for a little bit before disappearing into a different room to get back to his games.

Annalise continued to work on the fried apples. She used a wooden spatula to stir the pieces, allowing them to cook evenly until they were a golden color. She prepared a dish to place them in and then slowly began to fish the apples out of the oil and place them in the prepared dish. She continued like this for a bit. There were always apple pieces in the oil. Annalise moved between shifting which pieces were in the oil and between cutting up more apples. When at last the apple basket was empty and all the pieces had been removed from the oil, she moved the hot oil pan off the heat and allowed it to cool on the side counter.

Grabbing a separate bowl, she dumped sugar and cinnamon into it and stirred it up. Then she took the sweet topping and poured them all over the fried golden apples. Once she had emptied the sugar bowl, she pulled a fork through the apples, allowing the sugar to mix evenly throughout. Then she set it out on the counter near dinner, with a large spoon ready to dish out servings to the men.

Before the dessert even had a chance to cool, the men were streaming in through the door. Jamie ran just ahead of them and quickly joined Annalise at the side table in the kitchen where they always waited their turn to get food. "I'm so excited for the apples," Jamie said, his eyes glistening with excitement. She grinned at him, knowing that he was going to love them. Her thoughts went to Reid and she wondered if he would love them too. In a line, the men slowly filtered through the kitchen. They would grab a plate, dish up the beans and beef, and then reach the apples with surprise. Some of the men made room on their plates for the apples while the others headed straight to the dining room with a promise to return after they finished their food.

Before too long, the line had disappeared and only Wade remained in the kitchen as he dished up his food. Annalise fell into line behind him, getting a plate for Jamie and herself. "Hello miss, how are you?" Wade asked kindly.

"I'm doing well, thank you…" She hesitated before finally asking, "Where is Reid?"

Wade licked his lips as he added a generous helping of the apples to his plate, not seeming to mind when the items mixed together. "He's out in the barn," he said finally, turning to look at her. "The small southeast barn. There's a mother cow who's gonna give birth any day now and he's keeping watch over her."

"Oh," she replied. While the idea of another baby cow was exciting, she couldn't help but wonder if Reid was out there due to their argument concerning Carter. "Don't you normally take the first shift?" she asked.

He nodded with a small shrug of his shoulders. "Reid asked to take the first shift tonight. But don't worry, I'll relieve him for the second shift." Wade smiled at her and headed into the dining room with his plate. With a frown, she finished getting their plates ready and then beckoned for Jamie to follow her into the dining room.

She placed Jamie's plate at his regular seat before leaning over to talk close to his ear, "I'm going to bring a plate out to Reid. You stay here and eat well. I'll be back." Jamie pouted slightly before digging into his food, seeming to forget the conversation entirely. She left him there and walked around the table over to Wade, "Can you watch Jamie for a moment? I'm going to bring a plate out to the barn." He nodded back at her with a small smile before he took another bite.

Annalise headed into the kitchen and quickly prepared a nice plate for Reid. She carefully put a cover over it and headed out the door, hoping that she wouldn't have too hard of a time finding the 'small southeast' barn.

She wandered around the barn area for a bit before finding a small building in the general area that Wade had described. She approached it slowly and when she reached the large brown door, she knocked and then pulled it open, poking her head in. The back corner was lit by lantern light in the otherwise dark barn. She walked towards it, wishing she had brought her own candle. There didn't seem to be enough windows in this barn to allow the fading daylight in. As she walked through, her eyes began to adjust.

There were many barn stalls but not all of them appeared to be for animals. Some of them were filled with farm equipment and tools, most of which she was not able to identify. There were lots of metal, wood, and harnesses put together in strategic ways. She had always respected farmers and ranchers but seeing their equipment and knowing that she didn't have the slightest clue as to what to do with it helped her respect to grow.

She moved past the stalls and toward the very back stall where the light was coming from. All was silent as she approached and she wondered briefly if perhaps Reid was asleep or if he wasn't in the barn at all. But then she reached the stall and was surprised to find what she saw. The mother cow with an extremely large, uncomfortable-looking belly stood, eating some hay from her feeder.

Inside the stall, closer to the cow's feet, lying on the ground on a blanket in the straw was Reid. He was reclined, looking very comfortable as he read a book with the lantern placed behind him so he could see well. Frozen, she watched him and felt her heart swell. The light seemed to glisten off his hair and make his serious face that much more dramatic. He looked completely entranced in his book as he stared at it seriously.

A small part of her wanted to sit down on the blanket with him and cuddle into his arms as he read. Allow the low light and his warm body to draw her into a comfortable sleep. Annalise blinked hard and shook her head at the lapse of judgment that had wrongly enchanted her. She had vowed to herself to not be reliant upon a man and was going to do her best to not fall for Reid when he seemed so resistant to her. She wouldn't give her heart to a man who constantly threatened to turn her away and didn't want her to have Jamie in her life.

She stepped forward to the stall door and into the main stream of light from the lantern. After unlatching the door, she moved forward and placed the plate on the edge of the blanket. Reid looked up at her, his eyes open wide in surprise. The air was silent as she turned and headed back towards the stall gate.

Chapter Fourteen

All day long, the only thing Reid could think about was how unexcited he was to see Annalise that evening. He felt nearly betrayed by her in how she had let Carter in and given him information about the ranch and how they were doing. Reid had done his best to not let out the knowledge of the sick cattle. It had taken lots of stern talks with his workers to understand the importance of keeping their lips shut during their trips to town and even in their letters home.

Thankfully he never had to worry about the vet telling, but it hadn't even occurred to Reid to talk to Annalise about it. She never left the ranch and only sent letters to her friend back home. He hadn't thought there was much to worry about. But apparently, he had been wrong. The whole rest of the day he spent in a huff, feeling frustrated at both Annalise and himself. He was never very level-headed when it came to Carter.

For the past few weeks, this cow had been big as she got closer to reaching full term with her calf. But that day, Jeffery had noticed that her udders were starting to fill up, which meant that she would be going into labor soon. They moved her to the barn to keep her safe from predators and hopefully keep her stress level down during the birth. Then they had checked on her every few hours.

Right before dinner, Wade said he would take the first shift but Reid had quickly interrupted him, "You always take the first shift. I can get it tonight. Just make sure not to forget about me." Reid ended with a joke, hoping that Wade wouldn't read into his unusual actions. Wade eyed him for a moment and appeared thoughtful before finally shrugging and heading off to dinner.

While the workers and Annalise were busy getting their dinner dished up, Reid had snuck up to his room and retrieved a blanket and one of his favorites, *The Adventures of Tom Sawyer,* before heading back out to the barn. He admired the beginning of the sunset as he walked and then went into the building. The cow mooed as he entered the stall and she seemed to give extra thought to his presence before finally turning back to her hay.

Reid took a moment to clean the stall of any uncomfortable lumps of dirt or rock and then laid out the blanket and lantern and got settled. Even as he sat though, he couldn't quite get his mind to focus on the book. His thoughts instead returned to the events of the day and worried over the decisions he had made, wishing that he could go back and change a few things. With a shake of his head, he did his best to focus on his book, knowing that he couldn't go back and fix the past.

He read for a while before a movement at the stall door caught his eye. He looked up in surprise to see that a lidded plate had been laid down on the edge of his blanket. His gaze met Annalise who stood just a few steps away and a silence fell over them. Within just a slice of time, she turned out of the stall and started to pull the gate shut. "Wait," he said, the word escaping him before he had a chance to think it through. She paused at his voice and turned to look at him, still standing at the exit of the stall. He bit his lip before forcing out a sigh. "I'm sorry." Her eyes widened and she stepped forward slightly, still watching him. He felt his heart thud heavily in his chest and he briefly wondered if this was the right thing to do. With a small shake of his head, he pushed the worries away and continued to speak, "Carter is a large rival for me and my ranch. He's a land baron who's always had sights on my land and well, we have a history." Feelings of sadness, pain, betrayal, and more crept into Reid's chest as memories started to flow in.

"What kind of history?" she asked, her head tilted in what appeared to be genuine interest. She took a step closer, moving farther into the stall.

Despite her curiosity, he shook his head, not ready to discuss such a vulnerable thing with her. "When I saw Carter in my house..." he looked down, not able to meet her eyes, "...it just brought back a lot of bad memories."

They fell silent for a moment and the only sound was the cow chewing on her food beside them. Annalise broke the silence, "I'm sorry that I let Carter into the house... and that I told him about the sick cattle." Reid waved his hand in a gesture to dismiss her apology. He had forgiven her long before she arrived in the stall. "How is the mother cow?"

He blinked in surprise and looked back up to her. "She's doing good,. He nodded, happy both for the change in topic and her interest in the cow. An interest in the ranch and cattle wasn't something that he'd expected from a city girl. "I don't think she's quite ready to give birth yet, but she's getting closer." Annalise nodded. She stood awkwardly near the gate, not yet leaving, seeming like she wanted to stick around but didn't know how. He tapped his hand lightly on the blanket beside him. "You're welcome to come sit and watch her for a bit if you'd like."

"Okay, thank you," she replied, a small smile on her face. She slowly walked over to him, making sure to give the cow plenty of room, and then she leaned down and gracefully folded her skirt under her to sit on the blanket. Once seated, she turned to look at the cow and studied it intensely. Although

Annalise was seated on the other side of the blanket, he could feel his body getting warm, his cheeks heating up, feeling embarrassed by her closeness.

She had her arm out and her hand pressed into the blanket, supporting herself with it as she leaned back slightly. He looked at her hand and thought how, if he just leaned his arm out a bit, he could touch her hand and interlace her fingers into his own. He wondered how her hand would feel in his. It looked so small and soft. Recognizing his thoughts and how unwanted they were, he quickly shook his head, doing his best to focus on something other than Annalise. But then she spoke, making it impossible for him to do so.

"Would it be alright if I said a prayer for the cow?" she asked.

Reid frowned at the request. He had never heard of anyone wanting to pray over a cow. Would God even listen to a prayer like that? "I'm not sure that it's worth your time and effort," he responded, his mind still not made up. "Aren't there better things to spend a prayer on?"

She tilted her head slightly, her lips pursed. "I don't believe that praying for one thing takes away a prayer from another. There have been many times in my life when I felt lower than a cow. When I felt that I hadn't done anything worthy enough to deserve a prayer. Yet, my mother always prayed over me every night of her life. So as long as I have breath in my body, I will try to continue her work, praying for those who believe they are worthy of prayer, and those who don't."

He stared at her with admiration growing in his chest. "I will not stand in the way of your prayer, if that's what you want to do."

She smiled at him, put her hands together, and bowed her head. Seeing her movement, he bowed his head as well as she started to pray. "O Lord, protect this cow with Your kind touch. Grant her strength as she does your great work. Guard her and those who look after her, so that in the morning, everyone can celebrate this new life. Amen." At the end of her words, Reid allowed his head to lift and watched Annalise lift hers.

"Thank you for looking after my cattle and caring for them as your own." Her cheeks heated to pink at his words. He changed the subject, not wanting to embarrass her. "Your mother sounds like a wonderful person. Will I ever get the privilege of meeting her?"

Her smile turned down. "Unfortunately not. She died earlier this year, leaving me alone with Jamie."

"I'm very sorry to hear that. It must have been very difficult for you two." His mood dropped at the news and he felt cruel for bringing up any memories with this conversation.

"Yes," she agreed with a nod. "It's been the most difficult for Jamie though. Losing his mom at such a young age--"

"His mom?" he asked. "So, you are his sister?"

Her blush grew even darker. "Yes, he is my brother. I have never been with a man," she repeated.

He held up a hand in apology. "I'm sorry to think otherwise."

She shook her head quickly. "I wasn't very upfront in my letters. Lucy, my friend, and I were worried that you might not allow Jamie to come with me. We are all the family each other has. I must do everything I can to protect him. But I am sorry to have misled you."

"It's alright," he said with a shake of his head. "It seems like you've been doing a good job raising him, from what I can tell."

"Thank you," she smiled. He returned the smile and then was slightly started when he heard a noise at the other end of the barn like the door was opening and closing. He frowned, wondering who was coming, as it was not shift change time. Then faces appeared at the other side of the gate, Wade and Jamie.

"Sorry," Wade apologized. He looked first to Annalise and then to Reid. "He was doing fine and ate his dinner really well but then I made the mistake of mentioning the pregnant cow and well..." He held up his hands and made a big shrug.

"Is the baby here yet?" Jamie asked with excitement coating his words. At the sight of her brother, Annalise had already stood up and was walking towards the stall gate.

"It's not here yet buddy," Wade said while patting the boy's shoulder.

"Aw," Jamie pouted, his bottom lip sticking out slightly.

Annalise chuckled as she let herself out of the stall and closed the gate behind her. "I'm sure that you can come to see the baby once it's here. But for now, we have dishes to wash." She wrapped an arm around the boy and gave him a quick kiss on the head before they disappeared from sight, heading back to the house. Reid watched them go, once again impressed with the amount of love that was between them.

"Are you doing good, boss?" Wade asked. "I can always switch you if you'd like."

"No, I'm fine," Reid replied with a small wave of his hand. "I've got a comfy place to relax, a book, and now some food. What more could a man want?" Wade nodded his head, although he didn't look like he quite agreed, but then with a small wave, he was headed back out of the barn as well. With the sudden absence of people, Reid wished more than ever that Annalise was back on the blanket, talking with him once more. That was a much better way to pass the time.

Chapter Fifteen

A few nights later, Annalise was sitting in her room at the desk. A candle lit up the room and flickered shadows across Jamie's sleeping form in his bed. A few of the men had gone out to town that day and had returned with the ranch's mail. Among the bills and letters was a letter for her from Lucy.

Annalise had kept herself from opening it right away because she knew that she'd want to write a response back immediately even though she still had many things to do. So, with a great deal of patience, she had waited to look at the letter until everything had been done. Now that the chores and workers were taken care of and Jamie was snoring softly in his bed, Annalise opened up her letter. In looping black ink letters, Lucy had written:

"Dear Annalise, I'm so happy to hear from you. Things here have been going well since we last spoke. We have a few new girls which has lightened my load quite a bit. We've even started to become friends. If you were here, I'm sure you would have enjoyed their company as well. During our time off, we go on strolls together and pick flowers. Madam is still the worst but she hadn't been upset with me in a while which is pleasing. I'm sorry to hear about the hardships that you have been facing. Continue to be strong and keep putting your faith in God that everything will work out. He's led you and gotten you this far. Don't abandon hope. I'll be thinking about you in the days to come. You will be in my thoughts and prayers. Write back soon. Sincerely, Lucy."

Annalise let out a small sigh and laid the paper down on the desk. Normally reading letters from Lucy only brought her joy. And while she had enjoyed hearing from her friend, she couldn't help but feel lonely. She got out some ink and paper and quickly began her response letter back to her friend.

"Dear Lucy, I'm very glad that you've been able to find companionship and new friends. I hope that things continue to go well for you there. Thank you for your kind words and support. Since my last letter, things have gone smoother on the ranch. Reid seems to be calmer and we aren't having as many problems as before. There is definitely still room to grow, but I will keep trusting in the Lord to get us through this. Jamie has grown at least a few inches since we've left. I keep having to adjust his clothing so that he can fit properly. I believe that the country air has been really good for him. I look forward to hearing from you again. You'll be in my prayers. Sincerely, Annalise."

She blew gently on the paper, helping the ink to dry faster on the page. Once she was sure that she wouldn't smudge it, she folded it neatly and slid it into an envelope. Then she addressed the letter and added a stamp. Finished with her task, she left the envelope on the desk, blew out her candle, and climbed into bed. Sleep did not come easily. She laid awake, staring at the ceiling. Just as she had told Lucy in the letter, things were going well on the ranch, yet she couldn't help but feel like something was missing. What she wouldn't give to have someone to talk to. A face-to-face conversation.

Being the only woman on the entire ranch was more difficult than she had expected. While she was surrounded by people every day, she still felt so alone without someone to talk to. Perhaps she could attend a chapel service in whichever church was most nearby. She was sure there would be one in town. The thought of asking Reid about church made her shift uncomfortably in bed.

She knew he was not a religious man and yet she also knew that he would be the best person to ask. "Lord," she prayed quietly, "Please guide me so that I can find what is missing in my life and fill it. I want to be happy here. I *need* to be happy here. Show me your way. Amen." With a satisfied sigh, she snuggled farther into her bed. Finally, she felt herself drifting off to sleep, pleased that she was going to take action and work to help complete herself.

The next morning, Annalise got up and ready with a bit more energy in her step than the previous mornings. Jamie helped her prepare oatmeal for breakfast by standing on a chair at the counter and using a large spoon to mix all the ingredients together. Then they added hot water to the dry ingredients and mixed it some more. Once the food was ready, they got out bowls and spoons before setting out glasses for drinks. The men arrived at the house as they often did in the mornings, tired and cranky. In a single file line, they dished up their food and headed to the table to eat. After Wade got through the line, Reid was next. He grabbed a bowl, eyeing the food eagerly as he approached it. Annalise quickly got in line behind him, biting her bottom lip as she tried to think of a good way to open the conversation.

"Did you sleep well?" she asked while fidgeting with her spoon.

"I did. Thank you. Did you sleep well also?" he asked. He turned slightly toward her as he talked but mostly, he focused on getting his food.

"Yes, thank you," she replied. He handed the dishing spoon to her and she quickly got some food in Jamie's and her bowl. As she put the spoon down, she saw that he was already heading for the dining room. She gathered the bowls, gestured for Jamie to follow her, and hurried to the table after Reid. He sat down in his normal spot beside Wade and she seated herself beside him with Jamie beside her. After getting Jamie settled, she smoothed down the front of her dress and sat down. After forcing herself to take a few bites, she turned to Reid, who was eating quietly. "So, I know you don't pray much," she started. He frowned at her, leaving a bite of oatmeal uneaten on his spoon. "Well, what I mean is, I uh, I enjoy reading my Bible." He set down his spoon and fully turned toward her, his eyes narrowed and his mouth in a tight line. "I just," Annalise fumbled, "It's always nice to read and pray in a peaceful, religious setting."

"What you are trying to say?" Reid asked, one of his eyebrows raised.

"I didn't know if we had any places like that around here," she finished lamely.

His forehead scrunched up as he considered for a moment before answering, "I think there are many peaceful places on the ranch. The closest to the house would probably be one of the gardens. There's not normally too much noise there."

"Oh, yes, the gardens," she replied. "But what about-"

"Look, I know that you are religious and appreciate following God, but religion never got me anywhere," he said. "My parents believed in God and raised my sister and me to follow him, but then my parents got sick and died within two months of each other. So, you can believe what you want and do as you wish, but leave me out of it." His voice was stern but not cruel. Even though she hadn't figured out where the nearest church was, she let the conversation rest as it didn't seem to be something that Reid wanted to talk about. So, she allowed her focus to shift to the numerous other conversations that were happening at the table. But even as she listened, her mind spun in thought. She was sure that it wouldn't take much effort to find the church in town, if it had a steeple, it could lead her to it itself. The largest worry that hugged at her mind was the fact that she had never ridden a horse before and she had no idea how to drive a wagon.

The men finished with breakfast and started getting up. After piling their dishes in the kitchen, they made their way outside to start their daily tasks. Jamie still sat at the table with a mostly full bowl of oatmeal. "I'm not making anything else right now. You should really eat as much as you can." He frowned at the thought and stuck his tongue out while making a face like he was in poor health. She rolled her eyes and left him at the table, carrying the last of the dishes to the kitchen. She started washing the dishes and then putting them on the drying rack. About halfway through the dishes, Jamie entered the kitchen. With a frown, he handed her his empty bowl and spoon. She smiled at him. "Thank you."

"You're welcome," he mumbled, before running out of the room to where he kept his toys and books. Annalise allowed her mind to return to her desire to not be alone. To find community and comfort. To attend a church service or at least spend time in a sanctuary. It didn't seem like Reid was going to help make that happen. She would have to rely on herself, as always, to get where she needed to go. She briefly considered taking the wagon into town, but then she would need help hitching it up and permission to leave.

And would she need help driving it? The thought of trying to get the horse and the wagon to go where she needed caused her knees to shake and her stomach to grow upset. "What about just a horse?" she whispered to herself. There was no way she could get it saddled by herself. But if she got one of the men to do it for her? Her hands paused on the dish; the cloth suspended as she thought. If she could get someone to help her with the horse, she was sure she could do everything else herself.

She finished the dishes with vigor and swiftly cleaned up the kitchen. Leaving the room, she sought out Jamie. Through the window she could see that he was outside, digging in the dirt with a stick. While he was still occupied, she hurried upstairs to their room and changed into an older dress that she wouldn't mind getting dirty. Then she put on her bonnet and grabbed the spare change that she had, her Bible, and the envelope with her return letter to Lucy. Now ready, she headed back downstairs to retrieve Jamie.

"Where are we going?" Jamie asked as she hurried him along beside her. They headed toward the main stable where she hoped they would run into someone. Anyone but Reid and Wade.

"We are going... on an adventure," she replied. If Jamie was happy to come with her, things would be a lot easier.

His eyes lit up at her words. "Are we going to go find a river to swim in, or look for some wild animals?"

"We are actually doing something else. But first, we need to get a horse. Can you keep quiet about our adventure?"

He quickly nodded and they continued to the barn, entering the door. To her relief, inside was a stable hand who was feeding the horses that were stabled there. He had on his work clothes that were already covered in dirt and hay, though the day was not even halfway through. She recognized the freckled younger man with light hair and a shaggy beard from the many meals she had made, but she knew that they had never spoken before. "Wow, look at all these horses," Jamie said while wildly gesturing his hands.

The worker looked up and smiled at them. "This is nothing, you should see the horses we have out in the pasture."

"Would you be able to help us?" Annalise asked as they approached.

"Of course," the man said. "What can I do for you?" He brushed off the hay from his shirt, missing the big clump that was in his hair.

"I need to go to town to deliver this letter to the post office. Can you saddle up a horse for me?"

He frowned. "Frederick normally takes the mail to and from town every other day. I'm sure he would be able to take it for you tomorrow."

Annalise sucked in a breath. "Well you see, this is an important letter and I need to see to it personally. Should I ask Reid to help me ready the horse instead? I'm sure he would be able to help."

"Oh, well, he's very busy today," the worker said, biting at one of his fingernails. "I suppose I can get a horse ready for you. Did Reid say which one you should take?"

She shook her head. "He didn't say."

"Hm, okay. I'll probably get you Sundance then. He's a good gelding." The worker headed off into the back room to grab the tack. She breathed a sigh of relief that the ranch hand had decided to help her. But even though she was relieved, guilt gnawed at her chest. Sending that letter was not her primary reason for leaving the ranch, and she had misled the worker to believe so. A sigh escaped her and she fidgeted with the lace trim of her dress. Things would have been so much simpler if Reid had understood what she was asking that morning.

Before she could dwell on it any longer, the worker appeared from the storage room. His arms were full with a saddle, saddle blanket, and bridle. He walked over to a specific stall door and loaded the gear up on the edge of the wall. Then he went inside the stall and easily walked up to the large brown horse. A lightning bolt of fear shot through Annalise's chest when she looked at the horse that she would have to ride. She shook her head slightly at herself, wondering how she was going to be able to manage such a large animal. She had seen horses from a distance all her life, but she had never gotten the opportunity to ride one. She had no idea how successful she would be controlling the large animal and she knew from other people's accounts that horses could sometimes act unexpectedly. What might happen if she failed to control it?

At her side, Jamie pulled on her dress. She glanced down to find him looking very excited with a wide smile and his eyes shining. He pointed at the horse and then did a little dance. She couldn't help but smile back at him, even as fear tightened her chest. She patted her brother's back and turned to focus on the horse. The worker easily got the equipment on and ready. Faster than Annalise was ready, the ranch hand was leading the horse, Sundance, outside. He stopped the horse by a large log.

"You get on first, miss. Then I'll help the young lad up after you," he said. With a deep breath, Annalise approached the horse and carefully climbed up onto the log. Remembering how she had seen the men do it numerous times since living on the ranch, she put her foot into the stirrup, grabbed the saddle, and began to swing herself up. Unfortunately, she got sort of stuck on the way up due to her dress catching. While the worker held the horse still, she slowly wiggled her way up until she was finally properly seated with both legs on either side of the horse as a man would sit in pants. Looking confident and knowledgeable, Jamie climbed up onto the log and with just a little help from the worker, was able to climb up in front of her and get seated on the saddle. The worker handed her the reins and then carefully looked them over. "Is there anything else I can do for you?" he asked.

"No, thank you. You've been so much help already. We really must be going," she told him. He nodded his head in understanding before turning back to head into the stable once more. Taking the leather strip carefully in her hands, she slowly turned the horse toward the road that she knew would lead them back toward town. "Are you ready?" she asked Jamie. He nodded his head enthusiastically. Slowly, she pushed her heels into the horse's side and it started walking.

The sudden movement of it taking steps had her swaying unsteadily. She grabbed onto her brother and they held on, gripping tightly as the horse slowly walked down the road. They continued to walk for a bit, slowly getting the hang of the way the horse moved and how to properly sit on it without feeling like they were about to fall off at any second.

They continued walking for a while, slowly making their way down the lane. Now that she was more comfortable, Annalise dared to look around at the beautiful countryside. It was so different from the city and she couldn't have been more glad. Her decision to be a mail-order bride had been out of her obligation to take care of her brother and their need for a safe home.

On her train ride here, she had not even considered her own happiness and how it might be affected. Yet, she was happier then then she had ever been before. The country was beautiful, wild, and full of reminders of the Lord's power and grace. So, when she realized that she was happy, she almost felt bad, because she had only ever planned for their safety, and instead had found something even greater.

They walked for two hours at that slow pace and all of her body was beginning to ache although she was excited for the return home as she was beginning to feel more confident and knew that the ride would go much quicker. For now, she hoped that they would arrive in town soon or else they would have to stop somewhere else for them to get a break on solid ground. While she wasn't worried about getting off the horse, she knew that it would be much tougher to get back on Sundance and they would need some sort of step.

"My bottom hurts," Jamie said, echoing her own thoughts.

"I know," she replied. "We should be there very soon." Within the next ten minutes of riding, she began to see signs of life. The road became better maintained with many smaller roads branching off of it. And behind the treetops, she could see smoke and the tops of the tallest buildings in town. She kept her eye on the top of the tree line, searching the buildings there until she finally found it. "There it is," she called out when she spotted the top of the steeple sticking out. As she shouted, her heels pressed into the horse. At the sudden sound and movement, Sundance took off running with Jamie and Annalise clutching tightly to its back, screaming in terror.

Chapter Sixteen

Reid hammered at a fence post, nailing up the new boards. While he could easily get away with having his hired help do all the fence repairs, he appreciated the physical effort of it and often volunteered himself first for the job. Thankfully, his men never seemed to mind. As he worked, he thought about Annalise and their conversation that morning at breakfast.

Normally, she didn't talk too much to him during their meals except to ask questions about what he wanted her to get done throughout the day. He frowned at the thought of her religious questions. He couldn't help but be bitter when that topic came up. That was just how he felt about it. A sigh escaped his mouth as he gathered a few more nails to add to the board. Even though talking about God and religion made him feel poor, he knew that those things were important to her. "I vow to be kinder to her when these topics come up," he said aloud to himself.

Finishing up on that board, he moved on to the next. Pulling out the nails of the old, broken plank, he threw it down and grabbed a new piece of wood. As he worked, he considered the past. While both his parents had been avid believers, it was his mom who had worked to foster that belief in Polly and him. In the evenings when they were children, she would tuck them into bed. Dad would come in to say goodnight and then head back out.

But Mom would stay and pull out her old, crinkled Bible, and choose a story from it to read to them. He remembered how comforting it was to hear her talk. While he didn't always believe the stories that she read, as some of them seemed far too fantastic, he always appreciated the calm and safe feeling they would blanket him with. When he grew old enough to not share a room with Polly anymore, he still joined them for the bedtime Bible stories, always feeling happy and hopeful in the safe ritual.

Reid let out a sigh and set down his hammer, having finished nailing up the current board. He knew that he needed to go back to the house and talk with Annalise. She had been trying to have a conversation with him and he had mostly brushed her off. He needed to apologize for how rude he had been. With an ache in his back, he began to gather his tools and clean up his supplies, stacking them neatly by the fence for him to complete upon his return.

Then he called over Lycan who had been grazing nearby. After loading up all the supplies that weren't safe enough to leave by the fence, he mounted Lycan and they quickly headed back to the barns. As soon as Reid got his supplies put up, he road over to the house. Once he reached the front yard, he dismounted and allowed Lycan to have the freedom to graze in the area while Reid was gone. To his surprise, when he entered the house, everything seemed mostly empty. Most days by this time, she would be in the kitchen, starting the preparation of foods and materials for the lunch that would take place in a few hours. But instead, when he entered the kitchen, he found it completely empty. Everything from breakfast had been put away, but there was nothing else to indicate that she had been in there recently.

He headed upstairs to her room. The door was partly open and he knocked on it, even though he knew in his heart there was no one inside. Pushing it open the rest of the way, he examined the room from his spot in the hallway. Their clothes and other belongings were all still there and there didn't seem to be much out of place. Perhaps they had just gone out for a walk? Something inside of Reid knew the answer, he just had to figure it out.

Parts of their conversation that morning started returning to him. His thoughts began to click into place and he sprinted down the stairs and outside. Not bothering to fetch Lycan as he had wandered a bit, Reid ran over to the stables and quickly entered the building. No one was in there, but he did notice that one of the stalls was empty. Heading back outside, he pushed the door open quickly and nearly ran into James.

"Sorry, sir," the worker said, quickly stepping back and out of the way.

"James, have you seen Annalise? I was just looking for her."

"I have," he nodded. "She had me help hitch up a horse. I gave her Sundance as he seems to be the calmest."

"When did she leave?"

James pulled on his beard in thought. "A few hours ago I would say."

"Okay, thank you. Please let Wade know that I'm heading into town and will be back soon." Reid hurried around the ranch hand and sprinted back to where Lycan was munching on the grass near the house. He quickly mounted and tapped his heels into the horse and they took off at a gallop down the road to town. As he rode, he cursed slightly under his breath, allowing the wind to steal his words. He would bet money that she had headed off to find the church. She had indicated as much when they talked earlier and he had been too dense to realize it at the time. Truthfully, he was surprised that she hadn't tried to get to the church sooner. He should have thought about her religious needs, being stuck so far away from the town. His men were constantly leaving to get breaks away from the ranch and he had never thought to offer the same to her.

Lycan sped over the miles quickly. He moved easily, undeterred by the distance and pace. Reid's eyes scoured the road beneath them, trying to find any signs of Annalise and Jamie. He could follow the path forever, but if she had strayed from the road, he might miss her. Sweat began to gather on his face and leak down his back, despite the wind whipping at him.

As he started to reach the outskirts of town, he began to make out some figures on the side of the road up ahead. Slowing Lycan down he studied them. It seemed to be a woman sitting on the ground and a boy standing just off the path-- with no horse in sight. He restrained himself from believing it was them until he got close enough to make out the details of her face. Then his heart soared and he felt like he could fly. It was Annalise and Jamie. He reached them and pulled Lycan to a stop, dismounting quickly.

"What happened? Are you two alright?" he demanded. Annalise looked up at him from her place on the ground. Her face was very red and he noticed some dried tear streaks on her cheeks from where she had cried. Jamie looked fine and didn't seem to be hurt or upset too much other than having extra dust on his clothes.

"I'm so sorry," Annalise said, still on the ground. "It was such a silly idea to go out on our own. We never should have left the ranch." She sniffed, looking like she might start crying again.

Reid knelt down beside her. "It's alright. I should have realized that you wanted to go to church or attend a service. I didn't understand this morning. Are you hurt? What happened to Sundance?"

"Things were going so well, but then I accidently spooked the horse when I saw the steeple in the distance. He took off running and we both fell off of him. I'm so sorry but I've lost your horse." Tears began to fall from her eyes, leaving more streaks on her cheeks.

He took a deep breath before speaking, doing his best to appear as calm as possible. "It's alright. The townspeople know my horses. We'll get him back..." He looked her over, not really worried about Sundance who he knew would return. His heart only ached with concern for her. "Did you get hurt when you fell off?" He glanced between Annalise and Jamie.

"I'm okay," Jamie said. "It hurt when I fell off but it was mostly really scary when the horse started running." Reid nodded his head in empathy. He knew what it was like to fall off a running horse. Then he turned to look at Annalise, waiting for her to finally tell him what was wrong.

She let out a sigh and gestured with her hand, "I landed wrong on my ankle. It hurts to try and stand on it." She pulled up the edge of her dress to show him and he looked at it from where he was standing.

"It doesn't look too terrible but it does look like it is swollen and starting to bruise. But I have no medical training. We'll send for the doctor to take a look at you. But until then, let's get everyone back to the ranch." He leaned down and carefully picked up Annalise, his arms under her legs and back, and carried her as gently as possible. He stepped up beside Lycan and lifted her as high as he could. She grabbed the saddle and pulled herself onto it. She moved her hurt leg carefully, but still ended up flinching slightly at the movement She held herself with so much poise and she was still so contained and proper, despite her injury. He couldn't help but feel very impressed with her. With a shake of his head, he refocused on the situation, knowing that now was not the time to think about how pretty she was.

Once Annalise had settled and seemed comfortable, he helped Jamie climb up into the saddle in front of Annalise. As soon as they were ready to go, Reid started leading Lycan back down the path towards the ranch. It was a long walk back to the ranch. Reid felt sorry that they had to turn around and head back so close to town, but with her ankle injury, it was best that they got home to take care of it. Occasionally he would have Lycan move a bit faster as they made their way down a hill or had a flat stretch of ground.

But every time Reid would look back at the riders, he could tell that Annalise was in pain by the way her face was white and pinched and her body sat stiff and rigid. The movement of the horse was not helping much. They made their way in near silence with just the sound of Lycan's hooves on the path to listen to. Occasionally Jamie would start talking with Annalise about the scenery or animals that he saw. She would nod her head and answer back stiffly, trying to mask her pain from entering her words.

After what seemed like the longest trip back from town ever, Reid was excited when he saw the start of his acres. They were nearly home. As he approached the ranch, he noticed some of the workhands in the nearby field closer to them than the house. When they looked over in interest at the arriving horse, he waved over one of his workers. Jeffery soon arrived, looking curiously at Reid leading Annalise and Jamie on his horse. Without a word, Jeffery looked to Reid for instruction.

Reid gestured back towards town, "I need you to fetch the doctor. It's not urgent, but I would like him to come today if he can."

Jeffery nodded quickly. "I'll go get him." He turned his horse and cantered past them back toward town. They continued on their path to the ranch house.

"I'm sorry for all the trouble," Annalise said, sounding disappointed.

"You're worth it," he responded before blinking in surprise. Quickly he turned his head away so he didn't have to see what she thought about his statement. Maybe she hadn't even heard it at all. They continued in silence all the way until they reached the house. Reid tied Lycan to the hitching post so that he wouldn't wander and then lifted Jamie off the saddle and down to the ground. Jamie immediately ran away from them and threw himself into the grass, looking exhausted from all the riding. Much more carefully, Reid lifted Annalise and lowered her to the ground. Unable to bear her full weight, she leaned against him, holding tight to his arm.

She tried to hop beside Reid toward the house. The movement was awkward and difficult for her. After just two hops, she stopped to rest. "I'm going to carry you inside," he told her.

She hardly nodded before he picked her up, his arms underneath her legs and back once more. He easily carried her across the grass, up the porch and into the house, stepping across the threshold, the whole time trying desperately not to imagine her as his bride being carried through the doorway of their home. Jamie followed after them, watching curiously.

When they reached the stairs inside the house Annalise looked up at them with dread, even as he carried her. "Perhaps I can just wait downstairs for the doctor?" she asked. Reid took a look at them, noticing how narrow they seemed while he held her.

"If that's what you want," he said. "You could sit on the couch in the sitting room?" She nodded in agreeance and they slowly made their way to the next room over. He helped her get settled, getting a pillow for her to place her foot on at an elevated level and even offering to fetch a cold cloth for it.

"Something cold sounds good," she agreed. "But after that, you should probably get back to your work. I didn't mean to take up so much of your day."

Reid frowned but reluctantly agreed. He retrieved a cold cloth for her and then at her repeated instruction to focus on something else, he finally left the house to go and take care of Lycan before finding something to do on the ranch. Even as he walked away from the house though, he knew that he would rather be right back at her side, making sure that she was alright.

Chapter Seventeen

The ride back to the ranch had been long and painful. Annalise knew that Reid was walking them as carefully as he could and that his horse was really riding quite steadily. Yet every step sent a jolt of pain to her ankle. Despite the bombardment to her senses, she gritted her teeth and held her breath at times, to make it through the pain.

She felt decently embarrassed that he had needed to come and save her. In her mind, she had pictured Jamie and her leaving, riding to town to attend a church service, and then riding back before anyone noticed they were gone. Especially Reid. Yet they hadn't even made it all the way to town before he was coming to their rescue.

She sighed slightly to herself, wishing that she had done a better job. While it had been embarrassing to be found on the ground like that, she had been most worried about poor Sundance who had run off. While Reid hadn't seemed worried at all, she couldn't help but fret and wonder if the horse was doing alright.

When they finally made it back to the ranch, she felt so elated that she wanted to dance or perhaps cry. Instead, she did her best to remain dignified and allowed Reid to carry her into the house. As soon as she was settled on the couch and Reid had run out of things to do for her, she sent him away to go work, knowing that he had already missed so much from the time it took to retrieve her.

Throughout the time it took to get Annalise moved inside, Jamie had been hovering around them, watching closely but staying out of the way, which she appreciated. Even though

Reid had left, Jamie still stood at the edge of the room, looking hesitant and uncertain as he gripped his arms around himself.

She patted an open spot on the couch and he quickly shot over, sitting down beside her. "Are you doing alright?" she asked him. He frowned, pursing his lips, and shrugged. "Do you want to talk about it?" she continued. He shook his head 'no'. She wrapped her arm around him, trying to comfort him. They sat in silence for a moment before she started to talk once more. "I know that was supposed to be a fun adventure, but that turned out to be a little scary." She waited to see if he would respond, and when he didn't, she continued to talk. "You did so well with our unexpected dismount of the horse. And having to ride back once Reid found us. I'm very proud of how you handled everything today." She rubbed small circles on his back, trying to comfort without overwhelming him.

He turned to her then. "That horse went so fast. And then we fell down." His eyes were wide. "It made my tummy hurt."

"It was pretty scary," she repeated.

"Yeah," he said, his gaze landed on the ground. His lip stuck out slightly.

She let out a small sigh, not sure how to dispel his fear. "Maybe sometime when I'm feeling better, we can practice riding a horse around the ranch, and then we'll be better prepared for our next adventure."

"Alright," he agreed after a moment of thought. "But only if Reid helps us. He's really good at riding horses." A large smile formed on his face. "He came riding up to us with his horse going so fast. Even faster than ours ran."

She let out a chuckle. "Yes, that is true."

They sat only for a moment longer before Jamie leaped off the couch and while running out of the room, shouted over his shoulder, "I'm going to get a book for us to read." She soon heard his footsteps racing up the stairs. Alone for a moment, she leaned back into the couch, allowing herself to fully relax. A small gasp of pain escaped her from the slight movement of her ankle and she murmured a quick prayer to God through gritted teeth. "Thank you, Lord, for keeping us safe even as circumstances threatened to worsen. You kept us safe and looked after us. Please help my ankle to heal so that I may continue your work..." she paused for just a moment before finishing, "Thank you for sending Reid after us. Amen."

Annalise and Jamie only had enough time to get through one chapter in his book before Reid arrived back with Wade. "How are you feeling, miss?" Wade asked kindly.

"Despite my injury, I'm still feeling very blessed," she responded with a smile.

"The doctor should be arriving soon," Reid said. "We need to get you moved upstairs now." His voice made it clear that she wouldn't be able to argue her way out of this one.

"Alright," she agreed.

"Jamie, want to go play outside? I know of a place where we can find some great sticks," Wade offered. Jamie's eyes brightened up at the statement and he quickly left his book on the couch and followed Wade out of the house.

"That was kind of him," Annalise said.

Reid nodded before turning to the matter at hand. "You're going to need to swing your legs off the couch. Then I can help you walk and get up the stairs. Would you like me to carry you?"

She couldn't help but scrunch her nose, wishing that she wasn't in such a position. "I would like to try to walk... Perhaps if you have some sort of walking cane, I could--"

"No," he interrupted. "Unless you want one of Wade's handmade walking sticks, you're going to need my help. To be honest with you, I would really like to help you up the stairs. I know that you could probably do it on your own, but it is sort of my fault that you got hurt. Since I didn't take you in the wagon. I would like to be someone that you can depend on when you need help." He stared at her, waiting for her to respond.

Surprised and touched at his offer, she nodded. "It's isn't your fault that I got hurt, but I would appreciate your help." She did her best to swing her legs back over the couch so that she could stand up, yet every single movement that she made with her ankle caused waves of pain to roll through her body. As if tiny knives were attacking her foot, she gasped at each movement.

Reid remained where he was until she had gotten her feet back on the ground. He reached out to her, taking her arms gently, and helped pull her up to a standing position. She only put her weight on her good foot, yet as she was pulled into a standing position, black spots invaded her vision and she swayed slightly. He steadied her body with his own, waiting there for her. Finally, her mind began to clear and she looked at him. "I'm alright. Although I think one of Wade's sticks would probably be very helpful right now for my free hand."

His lips pursed. "If the doctor agrees, we can get you something to help you walk. But right now, let's focus on getting you to your room." He pulled her arm around his shoulders and wrapped his arm around her side. "Just try to not put too much weight on your foot."

She nodded, and they started the very slow walk down the hall and toward the stairs. They only took small steps, awkwardly making their way. They continued on like this until they reached the stairs. She looked up the steps with dread filling her heart. "Are you sure I need to be in my room?"

He sighed in response. "There are no bedrooms on the ground floor. That means that you won't have a private space for the doctor to attend to you. And he will probably order you to have some bed rest anyway. So, we will still have to get you up the stairs. In this situation, putting it off will not help with the solution. Only delay what we already need to do."

She grunted. "Well how do you suggest that we get up the stairs?"

"The same way that we walked over here," he responded evenly. They took the stairs even slower than before, but step by step they made their way up, slowly climbing to the second level. She was out of breath by the time they reached the landing and they stopped for a break even though the room was only a few feet away. Although she wished for a longer break, she nodded for them to continue and they made their way into her room. Reaching her bed, she carefully lowered herself down onto it and he helped her swing her legs up. She had just nearly settled when they heard the front door open.

"Mr. Shaw?" called a voice.

"Up here, Doc," Reid called back. Annalise frowned, wishing that she had been able to take more time to settle in her room after their journey through the house. She quickly shook off her disappointment and brightened at the thought of getting her injury fixed. Then maybe she could get started on lunch...

"Good day, everyone," the doctor said, reaching the entryway to her room. "I'm Doctor John Clemmens. What seems to be the problem, miss?" Doctor Clemmens looked at her through kind brown eyes. His neatly trimmed beard bordered his face. He was an older man who had seen many years come and go but he still seemed to be strong and in good health as he approached them with his medical bag in hand. Reid nodded his head at them and left the room, heading back down the stairs.

Annalise called after him, "Can you check on Jamie?" He nodded quickly and then disappeared from sight. The doctor stepped closer to her, waiting patiently. "I fell off a horse," she explained gesturing towards her foot. "My ankle twisted when I landed." Doctor Clemmens took his time examining it. He moved it this way and that and felt along the bones. While it was painful, she did her best to not impede his examination. But when he finally set her foot back down, she couldn't help but sigh with relief.

"It looks like a bad sprain. It will heal and return to normal but you will need to spend a few days resting. Staying off of it is the only way that it will get better. Plan to spend the next week in bed as you heal." He patted her shoulder gently and then gathered his medical bag and left the room. She remained on the bed, staring at the ceiling as her mind spiraled. How was she supposed to fulfill her duties here while resting? It wasn't possible. Slowly, she pushed herself up and carefully got her legs off the bed, and she was considering the best way to pull herself up to a standing position when there was a knock at the door. She looked up and immediately felt her cheeks growing hot to see Reid standing at the door, watching her.

"What are you doing?" he asked, watching her with careful eyes.

"I need to go make lunch for the men. And I need to check on Jamie, and I should probably do some washing if I have the time-"

"Annalise," he interrupted her gently. "I spoke with Doctor Clemmens. You are supposed to be resting right now. You need to stay put." She frowned at his words and continued trying to stand up. Reid watched her and continued talking. "Jamie is with Wade. They're becoming fast friends. It seems that they've made a sort of fort outside." She paused her efforts to stand, taking in the information. It was then that he leaned out into the hallway and grabbed something. Leaning back in, he held up a walking stick in a large smile on his face. "I had Wade grab this for me before taking over the care of Jamie. He's made quite a lot and usually just gives them out for free now. Now, just as you asked, you should be able to have more freedom and attention"

"Thank you," she replied, her smile genuine. "I'm glad that I won't have to fully rely on you but I appreciate how much you have already helped me."

"You just shouldn't have to carry it all by yourself, when you're healthy and when you're not. Please let me help you... You know, I am a pretty good cook." He smiled at her. She looked at him with surprise, her eyes widening and her mouth opening slightly. "What do you think we did before you came here?" he asked with a chuckle.

"I'm not sure," she replied quietly, realizing that she had never thought about it.

He looked down at the ground, seeming to study his boot with great intensity, then he spoke. "I had to do everything after my parents died." She felt her heart sink at his words, but she didn't dare speak, not when he was sharing something so personal. "It was just Polly and I. No one was coming to help. No one was going to save us or the ranch. I did the cooking and the cleaning, along with what I could maintain on the ranch. Polly tried to help of course, but she was just a child."

"You were just a child," she replied.

He looked up at her, "Not anymore I wasn't. Anyway, I'm no stranger to cooking for the household. I will take care of it, and I'll take care of you until you are back up on your feet." Her eyes widened and her hands started to get clammy. She'd had to escape her old life when she became too much of a burden, and now she was becoming a burden to Reid. Her mind raced as she started feeling emotionally desperate. If she couldn't pull her own weight, he wasn't going to want her anymore.

Instead of helping out with daily tasks, she was just going to be adding to them. What if he sent her back? What if he sent Jamie away? Would he drown her with work once she was back on her feet? Her fingers found the blanket on the bed and started to pluck at it nervously. Reid stepped closer to her and leaned down so that they were eye to eye. "The Bible tells us to care for the weak." Her mouth nearly fell open with shock at his words. But then he continued and started to quote, "I have showed you all things, how that so laboring ye ought to support the weak, and to remember the words of the Lord Jesus, how he said, 'It is more blessed to give than to receive'."

"Was that Acts?" she asked, wondering if she had fallen asleep and all of this was a dream.

His cheeks tinted red but he nodded. "Acts 20:35."

"You had it memorized," she replied, still feeling dazed. "How did you know it?"

"My mother," he said with a small nod. "She was very devout and taught me many things." He stood back up and turned, getting ready to head downstairs. But at the last moment, he faced her again. "The next time you want to go to church, I will accompany you." As he spoke, his face bunched up making him look worried and annoyed at the same time. Then he nodded his head and left the room, headed toward the kitchen.

Annalise couldn't help but sit in her bed for a bit, feeling a large amount of shock. The day had progressed so differently than planned, and yet in some ways, it had finished better than she could have imagined. Other than her ankle at least. She leaned forward and found that she could just reach the paper and ink on the desk. Pulling them to her, she got ready to write a new letter to Lucy. So much had happened since the night before.

Chapter Eighteen

Reid stood in the kitchen, fidgeting with the tie he picked out. He had stood in his room for over ten minutes trying to decide on the right tie to wear today. And he really didn't have that many options to begin with. When his father died, his tie collection had been something he kept, despite his lack of use for them. He had fond memories of his father wearing different ties to the church services every week, always working hard to be presentable when going to worship.

The tie he had decided on was a dark blue color that contrasted with his white button-down shirt. He had tied his tie with no problems as he always remembered how his father had shown him to. But now that it was on, he wondered if perhaps he should have gone with the light blue one. He let out a frustrated grunt and dropped the end of the tie, nearly placing his hands behind his back in an attempt to leave all the stifling fabric alone.

He missed his normal ranch outfit, but it would just have to wait. Loud sounds echoed from the stairs. He headed out of the room to see who it was and found Jamie, in a nice shirt, pants, and cowboy hat, as he raced down the stairs, jumping onto the first floor with a big clang. "Slow down there," Reid told him with a grunt. Jamie let out an excited laugh but Reid didn't even hear it as movement at the top of the stairs caught his eye.

He turned in surprise to see Annalise climbing down the stairs herself. "You shouldn't walk on the stairs with your ankle," he cried in surprise. He began to make his way up the stairs to her but she held up a hand. Hesitantly, he stopped a few steps away from her.

She let out a small chuckle with a shake of her head and continued to slowly walk down. "How else did you expect me to get down the stairs? You've had me on bed rest for an entire week. I haven't been allowed to do anything. But now that I've healed, I can do this." She reached where he stood and with a small nod, he backed up and out of her way so that she could continue on.

"I had just hoped that you would be taking it a little bit easier," he admitted. She finally reached the first floor with a little sigh at having made it down. Jamie raced over to her and gave her a big hug, large enough that he leaned back and his hat tumbled off his head. Reid quickly reached down, picked up the hat, and had it back on Jamie's head as he was finished with the hug. He then quickly looked away, hoping no one would acknowledge the action. Still facing ahead, he extended his arm out toward Annalise. After a moment, she took hold of it, and Reid couldn't help but let out a breath of relief. Slowly, they made their way out of the house and to the wagon that was ready and waiting just a few feet from the front door. Once Jamie had climbed in, Reid helped Annalise as much as he could to get her into the wagon safely. After a few tries, she finally made it up and inside of it, happily sitting on the seat. He closed the door, made sure it was secure, and then climbed up to the driver's seat, moving the reins and starting them on their journey to church.

They rode down the path and Reid's mind couldn't help but wander to the last time they had been on this path together, just one week before. He knew that the week of bedrest had been hard on Annalise, and not just because her ankle was in pain. Despite his best efforts to reassure her, she seemed to carry a lot of guilt for not being able to take care of the normal things that had been her responsibilities since she had arrived at the ranch. Even as he reassured her every day that he didn't mind making the food and cleaning up the dishes and house, she didn't seem to believe him.

But even Reid knew that the thing she felt the most guilt for was not being able to properly take care of Jamie the way that she saw fit. She did her best to keep him entertained in the room but even she knew when it was time to give up and let him roam. Reid and his workers did their best to keep an eye on Jamie and send him back up to her when he hadn't visited in a few hours.

Reid made sure to personally deliver all her food to her and to make other trips up to her room to check on her as well. With every day that passed, he had grown to enjoy the visits with her more and more until he looked forward to them. And while he should have been happy that she was now back on her feet and ready to start taking responsibilities back, he was also quite sad. Only having shared meal times with her didn't seem to be enough anymore.

But this, this he could do for her. If she wanted to go to church during her free time, he would gladly take her. So that she wouldn't get hurt or lost, yes, but also so that he could spend time with her. He shook his head, trying to get rid of his thoughts and not read too much into the emotions that had bloomed in him in the time that Annalise had been a part of his life.

The journey to town was simple and easy. They caught up to a few other wagons which Reid assumed were also heading to church. The morning sun had now risen high enough to start heating up the day and blind his eyes, but he didn't mind too much as they were just about to enter the town. They soon passed the town limits and began to ride past the first general stores and market areas. The church was near the center of town. Farther in than the saloon and not quite as far as the train station. They approached the plain white building. The most notable thing about the building was the large bell tower spire on top of it. He parked the covered wagon at one of the unoccupied hitching posts and quickly got down to tie up his horse. After pulling on the rope to make sure it was secure, he opened the door to the wagon and helped Annalise and Jamie climb out.

"It's beautiful," she said, turning to look at the white building in awe. He briefly wondered if he had ever seen her this happy before, but figured that he probably hadn't. Jamie and Annalise held hands and started heading toward the building. Reid followed close behind as he looked at the building through narrowed eyes. The closer they got, the more tightness he felt in his chest until he wasn't sure if he would be able to breathe once he got inside. Part of him wanted to interlace his hand into Annalise's empty one, but instead, he slid it into his pocket. They entered the building, falling into line with the trail of people who were also attending that morning. The pastor stood a few feet into the building, greeting everyone who entered before they found a seat for the sermon.

The pastor grasped hands with the couple ahead of them and then patted the man's back as they moved forward. He looked up to the next in line with his usual smile. But when his grey eyes landed on Reid, they grew wide and he tilted his head to the side. "Reid Shaw?" he asked, surprise laced in his voice.

"Yes, sir," Reid said, holding out his hand. They quickly shook hands while the paster let out some deep laughs. "Pastor Thomas, this is Annalise and Jamie Owens."

Pastor Thomas quickly turned to them, shaking their hands. "Are you all to thank for getting Reid down here? I've been missing his face around here, so I appreciate any part that you've played."

Annalise glanced between the pastor and Reid before turning back to Pastor Thomas. "Thank you for having us today," she told him. They moved past him and were able to see all the seats, available and occupied.

"Where do you want to sit?" he asked her.

"As close to the front as possible," she said, already leading the way up to the only empty seats at the front. He frowned but followed her up, only pausing to glance at the bench where his whole family used to sit. They finally got to their spots and settled in. The people sitting in the seats nearby looked at their group with great interest. He smiled kindly at them, feeling the heat rise on his neck and cheeks. Annalise and Jamie didn't seem to notice the stares, however, continuing to look around the building, taking everything in. He pursed his lips together, not wanting to mention all the staring eyes that might make her feel uncomfortable. He wasn't surprised that everyone was staring at him. Most of the people he recognized and knew by name. Living in this town all his life, he had grown up around most of them. And while he saw most of them regularly in the shop or when selling cattle, it had been many years since he had attended church. And he had never attended church with a woman and child.

The rest of the people, who weren't staring and giving them kind smiles while talking around the back of their hands, filed in and found seats. Once everyone was ready, Pastor Thomas made his way to the front. Reaching his podium, he quickly got started. "Thank you all for joining us today in this place of worship. We will begin with a moment of prayer. Please bow your heads... Oh Lord, thank You for Your kindness and love. We are here today to learn more about our relationship with You and what it means to truly love like You did and still do. Please bless us and guide us. Amen." The entire room echoed with 'amen' and then fell silent once more.

An older woman with white hair and a well-worn brown dress headed to the front left where a piano sat and she quickly readied herself to play. Everyone grabbed a hymn book from the shelves built into the pews and stood up. While Reid stood with Annalise and Jamie, he didn't bother to sing, but respectfully listened until the songs were done and the pianist left her instrument and returned to her seat.

Pastor Thomas returned to the spot at the front and cleared his throat. "Today we are going to discuss one of the most important lessons of the Gospels. While this idea is repeated many times in multiple books of the Bible, it is first clearly seen when Jesus is being questioned about the greatest commandment in both Matthew and Mark. The Matthew verse in chapter twenty-two goes like this, 'Jesus said unto him, "Thou shalt love the Lord thy God with all thy heart, and with all thy soul, and with all thy mind. This is the first and greatest commandment. And the second is like unto it, Thou shalt love thy neighbor as thyself."' Verses thirty-seven through thirty-nine." He paused and looked out at the crowd of people, allowing them enough time to think over what he had said.

"Now, what did Jesus mean by this? Loving the Lord thy God with all your heart, soul, and mind. That seems easy to me. We know that God sent his Son to save us so that we could go to heaven by believing. Despite being sinners and not deserving it, we get an eternal reward. God created this whole world for us and made us masters over the land and animals. I have a hard time coming up with reasons why I shouldn't love the Lord with everything that I have." He took a breath, allowing his gaze to wander amongst the people in the church before continuing. "I can see why that is the first of the greatest of commandments. And the second? Love thy neighbor as thyself." He shook his head. "That is much more difficult than the first, wouldn't you agree?"

"Pastor Thomas," one of the male members interrupted, "I have great neighbors and couldn't imagine loving them any less." A large anonymous chuckle seemed to sound from everyone present. Pastor Thomas nodded his head with a small smile and laughed as well.

"You're right, George; when we have amazing neighbors, we have no problem loving them and treating them just as well as we would ourselves. Yet, what about when we have neighbors that aren't quite as good? Maybe you have a rivalry with your neighbor. Perhaps they have wronged you by stealing your crops or gossiping about you. What do you do then? Do you still have such an easy time loving them?" The entire room was quiet and Reid himself felt a slight shiver down his back. It was always easy for him to love and take care of his workers. In fact, he didn't have a problem with most of his neighbors. But when it comes to someone like Carter, he wasn't sure that he was able to follow the commandments.

The pastor clasped his hands together in front of himself. "Loving someone doesn't mean that you like them or even want to spend time with them. You don't have to invite them to your wedding or write letters to them, but you still need to care for them. If they need help, offer a hand.

If they are hungry, give them food. If they need someone to listen to them, lend an ear. Loving someone is taking care of them despite how you feel about them. I'm going to take a guess that not everyone here likes themselves, and yet you still love yourself by eating food, spending time with friends, and finding a purpose in life. Love thy neighbor as thyself. That is the second of the greatest commandments.

Take some time this week to see how you can show love to your neighbor-- you might just surprise yourself with how much love you can show." The pastor continued on with his sermon for the rest of the hour. His voice was calming to listen to, yet Reid found himself growing more agitated and uncomfortable in his seat as he spoke further on loving enemies and neighbors alike. Halfway through the sermon, he glanced over and saw Jamie's head leant against Annalise's shoulder, his eyes drooping. For a moment, he wondered what it would be like to feel Annalise's head leaning against him, and his agitation faded.

The pastor's voice stirred him from his thoughts. "Now, let us pray." Everyone bowed their heads and closed their eyes. "Oh Lord, thank you for showing us your path and your purpose for us. For helping us to love you and to love our neighbors. Guide us in our actions that everything we do represents your love for us. Amen."

The crowd repeated, "Amen," and then lifted up their heads.

"Have a great week folks," he called out before moving away from the front of the room and to the door at the back to talk with people on their way out. Everyone began to stand and Reid, Annalise, and Jamie joined them. Then they started the slow walk towards the door, waiting for everyone ahead of them to make their way.

Annalise turned to him with a smile, her eyes seeming to dance and dazzle as she said, "Thank you so much. It feels so wonderful to be back in church and out of the house. I almost think that was the longest week of my life." She let out a chuckle.

He smiled at her. "I'm glad that you enjoyed yourself." They fell quiet and continued to slowly move through the crowd. As they walked, he realized just how comfortable he was spending time with her. She had made church worth attending for him and that wasn't something he could take lightly. He felt sad that they would be seeing each other so much less now that she was healed and things could get back to normal. Then an idea appeared in his mind and he turned to her. "Would you like to attend the cattle auction with me tomorrow? I'm sure Wade wouldn't mind babysitting." He smiled with amusement.

She looked at him in surprise. "I've never been to an auction before. Would I need to do anything?"

"No," he shook his head. "That's what all my cattle hands are for. You would just be there to enjoy yourself, get some time out of the house."

She opened her mouth with a large smile, seeming about to agree, and then her gaze dropped back down to Jamie who was walking beside them, not appearing to have noticed their conversation. "Are you sure he would be alright with Wade? I would hate to inconvenience him, especially if he was supposed to be helping with the auction."

"Nonsense." Reid shook his head. "He normally wants to stay home anyway and work on the ranch. I'm sure he would love the time off to work on building forts and fighting with sticks."

Noticing the conversation, Jamie looked up quickly. "I want to build forts and fight with sticks." The adults let out a chuckle.

"Alright," she finally agreed. "I would love to go with you." Reid couldn't hold back his smile as they left the church and returned to their wagon. The ride back seemed to go by in a blur as he looked forward to the next day ahead.

Chapter Nineteen

The next day, Annalise leaned forward in her seat, peering out the side of the covered wagon, waiting for a glimpse of the cattle auction. If Reid had been in the cart with her, she probably would have done her best to contain her excitement, sitting properly and making conversation. However, he was the one driving the wagon and no one else was inside it with her, so she allowed herself to lean against the side of the wagon wall, waiting to see the large set of barns appear.

Soon she would experience her first cattle auction. Since he had asked her to go with him to it, she'd had a hard time thinking about anything else. Once they returned home from church the day before, she had started making dinner. The ranch hands had been very busy the days prior, herding specific cattle to the auction so they would be ready for the big day and they were looking forward to a large delicious meal that night.

She stood on her feet for a few hours as she made cornbread and fried chicken. The men had seemed incredibly cheerful and thankful for her food and she wondered briefly if perhaps they were excited that she was back to cooking for them. But she dismissed the thought quickly, now having firsthand experience of how tasty Reid's food was.

By evening when she was getting ready for bed, she found that her ankle was aching from all the use. Once she had climbed into bed, she elevated it, with the hope that it would feel better in the morning. Even though she was comfy in her bed, and Jamie was sleeping soundly, her mind seemed to race too fast for her to fall asleep. She thought through her last week. It was the longest rest of her life, being required to sit still for so long. She was happy that the sprain wasn't worse or she feared that she wouldn't have made it any longer. After the first night of her trying to get around when Reid wasn't available, she knew that she wouldn't be able to make it the rest of the week like that.

Reid had kindly selected a number of the walking sticks for her to pick from that Wade had carved throughout the last few years. "These are lovely," she had whispered as she examined the many art pieces. "Can you tell him that for me?"

"You should tell him yourself. I think it will mean more," Reid had replied. She was in bed and after getting permission to enter the room, he had spread out the sticks across her bed before backing up to the doorway to wait patiently.

One at a time, Annalise picked up each stick, observing the fine craftsmanship. The sticks seemed to be made out of different types of wood as they were a variety of colors and weights. Seven some of the texture and wood grain seemed to be different. But the part that she found the most fascinating was the different designs that Wade had etched into them. Some had birds, others had snakes.

But her favorite was the one that little insects carved into it. Along the length of the wood, he had taken the time to carefully etch little drawings of bugs. The handle itself was designed to look like a large leaf. "Thank you for bringing these to me," she smiled at him. He shuffled slightly in the doorway and looked at the ground with a small smile on his lips. "I'd like to use this one," she held up the insect one, "as long as its height works well with mine."

"Would you like to test it? I can help you up," Reid offered.

"Yes, please," she told him, knowing that it would be painful and difficult to do on her own. Reid moved forward to her and gathered up the extra sticks, placing them beside the bed and out of the way. Then he extended his arm and took her hand, helping to pull her out of the bed. She balanced on her good leg and placed the walking stick on the floor, getting a feel for it. Finally, she let go of Reid's arm and took a few steps on her own, balancing against the stick.

"How does it feel?"

"It feels good," she replied before circling back and sitting on the bed, already feeling quite exhausted.

"Good, I will let him know which one you have decided on," he replied, gathering up the extra walking sticks.

"Please let him know that I will return it to him as soon as I can walk on my own again."

"Oh, I believe he intends for you to keep it," Reid said.

"I could never pay him for something like this," she protested, "I don't have enough money saved up."

"I don't think he wants money for it," Reid said, frowning.

Annalise held out the stick, now not wanting to take it. "Well, something that he spends so much time and effort on deserves to be rewarded. And I can't afford to pay him. Please let him know that I have respectfully declined the offer." She wiggled the stick, waiting for Reid to take it. He hesitated and then stepped away from her instead of toward her.

"I will purchase it for you. If you want him to be paid, then I will pay him."

"That's not what I meant. I didn't mean for you to-"

He held up a hand for her to be quiet. "Will this stick help you to heal? Will it be of use to you?"

"Yes," she finally said.

"Then I will purchase it for you." He smiled at her. "Now get some rest. And don't worry about repaying me, your healing and getting well is all I need in return." Then he turned and left the room with the extra sticks, pulling the door shut gently behind him. Annalise had sat in her room, mulling over the exchange while gratefully holding the wonderfully carved stick beside her in the bed. She thought as hard as she could but could not think of a greater possession that she had, other than her Bible. She fell asleep that night and many of the next memorizing the feelings of the bumps on the stick.

That week she was so grateful to have the walking stick that allowed her a bit of independence during her time of recovery. Now that she had recovered and didn't need it anymore, she still thought of it in the corner of her room and she looked forward to the next time she would get to use it. Being fully independent that day to go to church had been wonderful, despite her current soreness. She was able to fall asleep easily, not worried about how she would feel in the day ahead.

The next morning, she was very happy to find that her ankle was feeling much better. She stretched it before getting herself dressed and ready for the auction. Reid had warned her not to dress too neatly as auctions weren't the cleanest of places. She carefully selected one of her well-worn dresses that was still on the nicer side and got ready. Once she was done, she helped Jamie finish getting ready.

"So, you're leaving me here?" he asked, not feeling confident about their plans as she buttoned up his shirt.

"You're going to be spending time with Wade today. I'm sure that he has all sorts of fun things planned for you guys." Her brother pouted and crossed his arms in frustration.

She quickly pulled him into a hug, "I'm going to miss you too." After a moment, she released him from the embrace. He shyly stepped back before smiling and changing the subject. "Do you think Wade will show me how to fix a fence? I see the men doing that all the time."

"Well, you'll just have to ask him, I suppose," she said, smiling at him. They made their way down the stairs and found that Reid and Wade were waiting for them. "Have lots of fun," she told Jamie before kissing the top of his head. He quickly ran off to Wade without a fuss and they made their way outside the backdoor and out of sight.

"Are you ready to go?" Reid asked with a smile. She quickly nodded and they headed outside to the wagon that was waiting for them. After riding for a while in a different direction than what they had taken to get to church the previous day, they finally arrived at the cattle auction.

"Oh, wow," she whispered to no one as she watched all the people, barns, carts, and cattle that they passed by. Reid found an empty hitching post and quickly got them secured before coming to help her outside. The smell hit her immediately. Similar to how it smelt on the ranch, except much more condensed as the numerous amounts of cattle, excrement, and people were all gathered in one place.

"Let me give you a tour," he said, holding out an arm. She graciously took it and they started to walk together towards a barn where lots of people lingered. The closer they got, the more moos she could hear as the cattle talked back and forth. She could also hear another sound that she didn't recognize right away. It was a very rapid, fast sound as if a human was talking in a quick unknown language. Interested, Annalise nearly dragged Reid with her in an attempt to take a closer look. They entered the large barn and there were many seats circled around a large, gated area. The seats were all filled with people who held little signs in their hands which had different numbers on them. Everyone was watching the gated area with great interest and Annalise soon understood why. This is where the actual auctioning happened.

In the pen, a man led a cow around by a halter and line, turning it this way and that so the crowd could see all angles of it. The large cow walked steadily with him, its brown tail swishing away flies that bothered its legs. On the other side of the pen was a small stage and a single man stood atop it. His words flew through his mouth in a repetitive, rumbling sensation. Occasionally Annalise could make out words like 'hundred' and 'Can I get a...' With every word he spoke, one of the people sitting outside the pen would lift their numbered sign and the man would point out the number and increase the bid in his babbling voice. Different numbered signs hopped up here and there, jumping around like the light from fireflies at night.

"This is amazing," she told Reid. He leaned down to hear her properly in the loud barn. She then glanced around, realizing that she only saw the one cow. "Where are the rest of the cattle?" she asked him. He nodded his head toward a door and they walked arm in arm out of the barn.

"That was the main auction hall. There is another one over there." He gestured toward another barn that was close in distance. "But," he said as he continued to lead them, "all the cattle are kept in these stalls." They walked into a large barn and it took everything in her to keep her mouth from falling open. As far as she could see there were stalls lined up and filled with cows and bulls. They walked between the stalls.

Groups of people lingered together in little makeshift camps of chairs and other items at occasional intervals along the stalls. "What are all these people here for?" she asked quietly.

"They are the owners or caretakers of the cattle in specific stalls. They ensure that the cattle are taken care of as well as they help walk the cattle out to the action hall or to the outdoor pens after sellers have purchased their livestock." As he explained, they continued walking and as he finished talking, Annalise realized that she recognized some of the people that they were nearing.

"Oh, greetings," she said pleasantly as the workers recognized them and started waving. There were five cattle hands from their own ranch who were doing just as Reid had explained.

"Jeffery is getting a cow ready to walk," one of the men gestured behind them toward the auction hall they hadn't visited.

Reid nodded in understanding. "Did the transporting go smoothly?"

"One of the yearlings twisted his foot while getting through the ditches. He's with the vet right now," a ranch hand responded. Annalise glanced at Reid to see how he would take the news, but he didn't seem surprised as his facial expression remained just the same as it had been.

"No other injuries?" he asked. The worker shook his head. "Alright then, carry on." At his word, the men returned to their activities. Some of them were eating food they had packed. Others started gathering halters to get the next group of cattle ready for auction. Reid let her over to the fence where they could get a good look at the livestock they'd brought.

"This isn't all your cattle," Annalise observed. She saw that only a small fraction of his herd was here. "What determines the cattle you bring and those you leave behind?"

He gestured his hands widely at the cows in front of them, "This is a variety of the very best of my herd. Because our finances are steady, we can afford to just bring the cattle that will earn the top bid from buyers." She noticed the pride in his voice as he spoke and the shine in his eye as he looked at the different cows. They turned when they heard new voices and saw that a few men, most likely buyers based on their nice outfits, were walking down the open row, examining the cattle with interest.

"Mr. Shaw, fine cattle as always," one of them said.

Reid tipped his hat at them with a smile on his face, "I expect you to be buying them, Mr. Lewis." They all chuckled and made small talk for a moment before the buyers continued on their way to the auction hall. Reid and Annalise stood in silence, enjoying the atmosphere. She looked around, absorbing all the details when she noticed a familiar face had caused her back to stiffen and her stomach to sink. She quickly nudged Reid and tilted her head in the direction he should look. His gaze followed hers and then quickly darkened. Down the row, walking toward them and pointing was Carter.

They watched as Carter stopped and talked with buyers, seeming to gesture toward Reid's cattle while whispering behind his hand. Some of the buyers looked up at Reid's area, their faces disgusted, and then turned away, moving in the opposite direction. Reid's eyes narrowed as he studied these situations. Carter continued this pattern, moving down the row and turning customers away from their cattle every chance he got. Suddenly one of Reid's ranch hands zoomed around Carter, nearly jogging over to them. "He's spreading rumors about us," the man said. "Carter is telling the buyers that your cattle were sick just a few weeks ago and are still contaminated." An angry grunt sounded from Reid and he glared down the line. But Carter was already heading to them, not giving Reid a chance to respond or dispel the rumors.

Carter had nearly reached them when Annalise noticed the woman on his arm. As soon as the young blonde woman was in sight, Reid stiffened beside Annalise and a small breath seemed to hitch in his throat. The woman attached to Carter was wearing an extravagant wine-red dress that had many shining beads sewn into its fabric. It was beautiful, although something Annalise would have expected to be worn to a ball, rather than a cattle auction.

"Afternoon, Miss Owens," Carter greeted. "I'd like to introduce you to Miss Laura Neville."

"How do you do?" Annalise asked the woman, nodding her head. "Are the two of you business partners?" she asked, knowing that this was unlikely.

Carter frowned before flashing a smile once more, "This is my new partner. But Reid already knew that." His gaze cut toward Reid who shuffled slightly on his feet, looking anywhere but the couple. Annalise leaned closer to him and slipped her hand into his. To her surprise, he didn't push it away but seemed to take it gladly. Then Carter patted Laura's hand and they continued walking, moving past them. As Carter and Miss Neville disappeared into the crowds of people who had resumed walking toward the Shaw cattle, Annalise glanced up at the man beside her, wondering at his reaction to Carter and Miss Neville. But he didn't meet her eyes and instead turned to help his workers get some cattle ready for auction.

Annalise noticed the change in Reid throughout the rest of the time at the auction but she did her best to not mention it. Once he was done helping his workers, he took her outside the barns to show where the cattle went once they were bought. There were large sets of makeshift stalls that were much smaller and seemed to be temporary in their construction. "As soon as the buyer pays at the main desk, he can come pick up the livestock that he purchased. But if he doesn't have the correct paperwork, then he can't get anywhere with them," Reid explained.

"Do they stay in these very long?" she asked, pointing to the small stalls.

Reid quickly shook his head. "No, they only get moved here once they're paid for, then the new owner gets to collect them."

They continued to walk around the auction, going and looking at wherever Annalise was interested in. She saw that there were a few vendor stalls set up and people were selling food out of them. Reid noticed her line of sight and quickly tugged them in that direction. "What are you hungry for? My treat," he told her.

"I don't want to impose," she told him, doing her best to look away from the food.

"Pick something out for us to share and we can call it even." He smiled. She grinned at him eagerly and they headed over to the vendors.

"What is that?" she asked, pointing out some small brown blocks.

"That's fudge, I believe. Would you like some?" She nodded and he quickly headed up to the stall worker and got a small bag of chocolate fudge. He returned to Annalise and they continued their walk while eating small bites of fudge.

"This is delicious," she told him, already making plans to bake her own at the ranch.

"I'm glad you like it. I'm also glad you're having a nice time at the auction. I am surprised that you have never been to one before in your previous town. I'd imagine that even small towns would have auctions, just smaller ones.

Her cheeks pinked slightly. "I'm sure our town had something, but my mother and I worked constantly with little time off, so we never were able to really enjoy the things our town had to offer.

A frown formed on his face at her response. "If you weren't able to get into town during your time off, then what would you do with your free time?"

"On our day off, we would go to church to worship, but once we were back where we lived, I would spend as much time as I could in the small garden out back. I would always spend some time harvesting any fruit or vegetables and weeding some of the unwanted plants, but my favorite part was always the bugs." He tilted his head to the side at this. She continued with a shy smile, "The bees, butterflies, and dragonflies first got me interested. But there are so many little critters in the dirt and living amongst plants. Some can fly while others crawl or walk on tiny legs. I find them so fascinating. I used to keep a journal with all my notes about the bugs, but then it was destroyed by the woman we worked for." She looked down at the ground.

"I'm sorry that happened to you," he told her gently. "Your fascination with the world of the small creatures is a wonderful thing. Have you gotten to spend much time outside since being at my ranch?" She shook her head no. "Well," he chuckled, "I think you will be pleased to find that the country has a lot more bugs in it then the city does. The next time you have a spare minute, you should take a look at some of them."

The smile returned to her face. "I do have some paper, perhaps I can start taking notes on them again." They started heading back towards the wagon. As they walked, he pointed a few other things out to her about the auction, but mostly he listened to her excited chatter about all the bugs she was going to see.

When they finally reached the wagon, the long day seemed to finally be taking its toll on Annalise as she became quieter. She was sad for the day to be over but she knew that Jamie would be missing her. She also figured that Reid didn't want to run into Carter and Laura again and they risked that happening the longer that they stayed there. She only hoped that at some point she could fully understand why they were opponents in the cattle business and why Carter always seemed to be so mean.

Chapter Twenty

Reid and Annalise were headed back to the ranch, driving the covered wagon home. While Annalise had seemed fine riding inside the covered wagon on the way there, she specifically requested to ride in the front seat with him on the way back and claimed that she 'wanted to see the better view.' Reid had frowned at this but didn't have a good reason to tell her no, so he had agreed for her to sit with him.

He felt disappointed about how the day had ended. He had been so excited to spend time with Annalise, showing her a part of his world. And she had seemed just as excited to be in it. Sometimes when his workers asked him lots of questions, he would start to get frustrated. But today, he had found that her questions hadn't made him feel the same way.

But then Carter has shown up with Laura. Reid's stomach turned in a sickly fashion at the thought. Not only that, but Carter had also been spreading lies about his cattle. He would never try to sell cattle while still sick and contaminated. All of the cows that had been brought had been checked by the vet to make sure they were in top condition for buyers.

The wagon wheels bumped along the rutted track causing it to hop up and down. Annalise fell over slightly and into him at the rapid movement. She quickly leaned up and away from him, her cheeks getting red. He smiled slightly at her reaction, despite his bad mood. But even Annalise's cute response couldn't keep his mind from returning to Laura. He thought about how that dress had really suited her, even if it wasn't the proper attire for that location.

"Who was that woman?" Annalise asked, breaking into his thoughts. He let out a long sigh. Laura wasn't someone that he talked about to anyone and normally, he wouldn't have answered. But it was different with Annalise. He felt comfortable with her and wasn't worried about her betraying his trust. But more than that, he didn't want her to misunderstand how he knew Laura.

"Laura was my fiancé," he said. His hands began to fiddle with the reins of the horse. "Four years ago, we were young and in love. Well, at least I thought we were in love. I proposed, she accepted, and everything seemed to be right with the world. At that time, I had hit my first successful stride. The ranch was doing really well and I was able to afford some more land and workers. A lot of people claimed that I had the most successful ranch in the area. But then Carter started to become a solid opponent. His business grew and so did his name."

Reid looked out at the landscape as dusk started to settle over them, the colors of the land becoming muted in gray. The warmth of the day started to seep away and all the night creatures started to make their appearance. Owls and bats flew through the air. Lightening bugs flashed throughout the trees and crickets started to sing their songs.

"What happened after that?" Annalise asked gently. Then just as quickly she said in a quiet voice, "You don't have to explain if you aren't comfortable."

"No, it's fine," he assured her. "After that, Laura left me for Carter. At the time I thought the only thing she had taken from me was my heart and a ring. But those weren't the only things she stole… Over the next few weeks, I discovered that she had taken the deed to one of my newest land purchases, my banking information, information concerning the sales and purchase of my cattle, and the contact information of the customers."

"Oh, my," Annalise said, her voice sounding as sad as he felt.

"Yeah," he agreed. "I'm just thankful that she wasn't able to find the rest of my deeds for the land our house and barns are on, as well as most of our pasture lands. But she took everything else. She took it all and gave it to Carter. They ruined everything that I had built up and did everything they could to destroy my image, business, and success."

"But it didn't work," Annalise said. "You seem incredibly successful. And you said so yourself that you are financially stable enough to only bring the cattle that would get the best price from buyers."

"Well, it's been four years," he reasoned. "A lot has changed in that time. Where you are now is not where you were four years ago, is it?"

She frowned and grew quiet as she thought. "I was also in a very different place," she finally agreed. "How bad did Carter and Laura make things for you? Did you have to fully restart?"

"Thankfully not. They tried to steal the land out from under me. And they had the deed, so that wasn't too surprising. But thankfully the bank wasn't a fool to listen to their stories, even with Carter trying to buy my mortgage for double what it was worth."

"You never gave up, did you?" she asked.

"No," he said. "It did cross my mind a few times though. Although the bank didn't betray me, we still almost went under. They stole nearly all my clients and improved their own business practices based upon my own." They fell silent before he started to speak again. "In those years, I would bring all my cattle to the auctions in the fall, in the hope that I would make enough money to survive the winter. I had to let go most of my workers and we could hardly afford to buy soap and sugar those days."

"You've come so far in such a short amount of time," she said, her voice in awe.

He smiled at that thought. "It definitely wasn't easy, but we did survive."

"There's a Bible verse that I really love to turn to when I'm in need of strength, 'The Lord is my shepherd; I shall not want. He makes me look down in green pastures. He leads me beside still waters. He restores my soul.' That's from Psalm 23:1-3."

"My mother often quoted that one when my sister and I would have bad dreams at night." He smiled at the memory. They fell into silence once more and watched as the sunset filtered through the trees. "Do you feel betrayed, now that I've truly told you about Carter? I'm sorry that I didn't tell you sooner."

She shrugged easily, not seeming upset, "We all have dark things in our past. But we do seem to be stronger together." They smiled at each other. They were nearly back to the ranch; their day out was nearly over. Annalise seemed thoughtful as they rode. "Carter seemed to be causing more trouble today, spreading false rumors about your cattle," she observed. "What are you going to do about it?"

"I'm not sure," he replied honestly. "But I've been rebuilding myself long enough now that I think I can handle a few lies." He turned to look at her, only occasionally glancing ahead to make sure the horse was staying on the trail. "I don't care much about what people think anymore. I've got enough blessings in my life that I am able to take care of my workers and provide some good beef to the community." He ran his hand through his hair under his hat. "The main reason I told you all of this is because I wanted you to know. You're becoming uh, very important to me," he said, his voice cracking slightly. "I know we didn't hit it off really well at the start but I want you to know that I appreciate having you here. You've come to mean a lot to me." His cheeks felt like they were on fire and he glanced away from her enchanting green eyes.

"You mean a lot to me too," she replied. He glanced back at her in surprise but then he smiled, knowing that she was telling the truth. The horse turned off the main trail and onto their property road. Reid was mentally pleased with himself and his horse for knowing which way to take them. Annalise interlaced her hand with his and leaned her head against his shoulder. At first, he couldn't help but feel nervous, his hands starting to sweat as he sat up iron-rod straight. But as they drove past the fields, he allowed himself to relax beside her, his hands loosening and his back curving. The horse continued past the house and stopped at the barn doors, waiting for Reid to unhitch him.

Although he knew he should get up and get started, as the daylight was almost gone, he had no desire to ruin the feeling of closeness with Annalise. She hadn't moved either, and he suspected that she felt the same way. He turned his head toward her and she looked up at him. Their eyes locked for a while and he examined how they sparkled, the way her nose curved along her face, how tiny freckles were just visible. She smelt of fresh soap and clean laundry and a flower fragrance that he couldn't name. Then he looked at her lips, their curved shape and pink color. He leaned closer to her and she tilted her head up to him. Their lips had nearly met when a loud call sounded behind them.

"Annalise, you're back!" cried Jamie. Reid and Annalise jerked apart from each other and turned sheepishly to look over at Jamie who had arrived. "How was the cattle auction? Did you get to see so many cows?" he asked quickly, nearly jumping up and down in excitement.

She let out a laugh and before Reid could move to help her, had started climbing down to the ground. "It was really great. I'll tell you all about it," she said smiling. He eagerly led the way back to the house and she followed him at a slower pace. Reid's eyes didn't leave her for a moment. And just when she was about to be out of his sight, she turned around and waved at him with a flash of a white teeth-filled smile. He quickly waved back with his own grin and then she disappeared into the night.

Feeling many pounds lighter, he got the horse unhitched and brought him to the pasture for him to graze on grass and rest. He eagerly tossed his head, seeming impatient with Reid's slow walking. But they reached the gate and quickly released him. Reid headed back to the barn and finished putting away the wagon. There were a few more end-of-the-day tasks to complete before he could fully relax. Normally his ranch hands would take care of them but with some of them at the auction, they were short on helpers.

So, he moved the last of the cattle to the barns and fed all the stabled animals before he headed back to the house. Wade had already taken care of dinner and some was placed off to the side in the kitchen for Reid. He grabbed his plate and a drink and then headed out to the front porch to eat in the company of the stars.

Wade soon joined him and nudged him in the side. "How did things go today?" he asked.

Reid pretends to think for a moment before answering. "Well, all the workers seem to be doing good with the cattle. We had sold nearly half the livestock that we brought there. I think it will be successful for us, once again."

Wade elbowed him harder. "You know what I meant." They both had a good laugh.

"It went really well," Reid told him sincerely. "I think she had a really great time. She couldn't seem to get enough looking at everything. The only negative thing was that we ran into Carter and Laura. It seems they've been telling people that I brought contaminated cows to the auction."

A growl sounded from Wade. "That bully always seems to be trying to cause trouble. Hasn't he made enough of that for one lifetime?"

"Apparently not," Reid replied with a sigh. "But on the ride home, I got to talk with Annalise about all of it. And she wasn't upset or hateful. I think she seemed really supportive of me."

"I'm really happy for you, boss," Wade said.

Reid smiled widely, "I'm really happy too. In fact, I think this is the most positive thing that has been for me in many years. I can't wait to see what tomorrow holds." They fell into a comfortable silence as Reid finished his food and drink and then they just sat, enjoying the evening air. The smell of cattle, ripening apples on the tree, and Annalise's fragrance on his sleeve warmed him. As Reid considered calling it for the night and heading to bed, he noticed a new scent in the air. The smell of rain seemed to be coming from the south and heading in their direction.

Chapter Twenty-One

Annalise stood in the kitchen, working at the counter. She measured out yeast, flour, shortening, water, sugar, and salt in a large bowl. As she mixed it, she hummed a sweet chorus of her own design, her hips swaying and her fingers tapping to the beat. Sunlight filtered through the windows and lit up not just the bread mixture but Annalise herself. She felt like a butterfly, fluttering throughout the kitchen, flying by her heart's beat.

In the bowl, she mixed all the ingredients until they were cohesive and then poured it out onto the floured counter. Grabbing the rolling pin, she pushed out the dough. Her forearms burned with the exertion but she didn't mind even as sweat started to gather on her forehead. Finally, the dough was long and elastic. She picked it up and set it into a bowl on a safe spot on the counter. Leaving it there, she began to work on cleaning up.

Gathering her measuring instruments and dirtied bowl, she brought them over to the wash bin and placed them inside the water to soak. She quickly washed her hands and then headed out of the room to peek at Jamie. He sat at the table working on a drawing, his pencils scribbling fiercely, his brow lowered in deep focus. She smiled at the sight of him and then turned back to the kitchen to finish cleaning up. As she wiped down the counters, she thought about her time with Reid on the day of the cattle auction.

He had opened up to her so much, much more than she had ever thought was possible. She really felt like he'd showed her a large piece of his heart. He told her about Carter and Laura, and even talked about his mother. Never in a million years had

Annalise expected Reid to share a Bible verse with her. They had quoted them to each other like the best of religious friends. This was not something she had even dreamed could happen. Yet here it was.

Her heart felt like it might dance right out of her chest like a grasshopper leaping through tall plants. She was amazed at these feelings and she had a hard time remembering an event prior to this one that had made her feel so wonderful. She carried on cheerfully away from the counter and to the dishes. Scrubbing at them, she allowed her mind to wander to the future. This was the brightest it had ever seemed and she couldn't help but dream about how wonderful it would be if the last few days were any indication. Lucy was correct in her letters; God did have a plan and knew what He was doing when He had Reid and Annalise cross paths.

She was nearly finished with the dishes when she heard a knock at the door. It was such an unexpected sound that Annalise's hands froze in place, soap bubbles dripping off them. She listened carefully, waiting to hear if there would be any more knocks. Perhaps she had imagined it? It was only Jamie and her inside the house as Reid and the workers were busy on the ranch. *Thud, thud, thud* came the sounds again.

Annalise quickly dried her hands on her apron. Her stomach felt like it was in knots as she walked away from the kitchen and to the front door. The last visitor she had dealt with was Carter. Her hands shook slightly as she wondered if it would be him at the door once more. She steadied herself and then grabbed the handle with certainty, opening up the door in what she considered to be a brave way. To her surprise, rather than Carter at the door, she found a sobbing Laura, Carter's wife and Reid's ex-fiancé.

"I'm so sorry to show up like this," the blonde girl sniffed. She continued in her scratchy voice, "May I come in?"

Annalise hesitated, studying the woman. Her face was blotchy and her eyes were red with tears threatening to spill over. The green dress she was wearing had become very dirty along the bottom. She glanced past Laura and couldn't find a wagon or horse of any kind. She briefly considered turning her away and simply closing the door, claiming that she was unavailable or ill or some other acceptable excuse. However, she remembered Pastor Thomas' sermon about loving thy neighbor, even when it was difficult. This must be one of those difficult times.

"Of course," she finally answered pulling the door open wider for Laura to enter. Mrs. Johnson stepped past the threshold and a small cry came from her throat. "Would you like some tea or some other beverage?" Annalise asked.

"That would be wonderful," Laura answered, her bottom lip nearly sticking out. Annalise led her guest through the house and to the kitchen. She quickly put the kettle on to heat up some water and then led Laura to the dining room for them to sit and wait. Jamie glanced up as they walked in, but just as quickly returned his focus to his drawing. Both the ladies found chairs and a silence fell over them. Annalise's mind ran in circles, trying to come up with something appropriate to talk about but she was finding it quite difficult. The kettle screeched, allowing her to get away from the awkward silence for a moment.

She hurried back to the kitchen and got two mugs ready along with tea leaves. After pouring in the steaming water, she carried the cups back to the dining room table and placed one in front of Laura, keeping the other for herself. They both stirred their drinks until finally, Laura began to speak.

"The reason I've come is, well…" Her eyes welled up. "My heart is broken." Annalise eyed her guest respectfully but stayed quiet, uncertain of what to say. Laura continued, "Seeing Reid at the cattle auction… I've treated him so horribly. I am desperate for his forgiveness, I can't hardly sleep at night and I toss and turn, thinking about what he had to go through."

"Whenever I'm feeling like I made a mistake or have hurt someone, I often pray about it to help clear my mind," Annalise told her.

Laura shook her head. "I don't think God wants to hear from me."

Annalise pursed her lips in thought. "Would you like to talk to Reid about it? I doubt that talking to me is what you really need to feel better."

"That's true," Laura sniffed. "I never did catch your name at the auction. And he is just the cutest," she said turning to look at Jamie. "I don't think I've ever seen you two around these parts."

"I'm Annalise Owens and this is Jamie." Annalise stood to walk behind his chair, putting an arm around it. Jamie looked up from his drawing, hearing his name.

"Owens?" she asked, an eyebrow raised.

"Yes."

"Is he your son?" Her gaze didn't leave Annalise as she waited for a response. Her eyes pierced straight through Annalise. All the trembling in her lips and hands seemed to have disappeared as she took a very slow, thoughtful sip of her tea.

Annalise quickly stepped forward and helped Jamie out of his chair, holding a protective arm around him. "We're going to get Reid for you. Wait here and he'll be right in. It was nice seeing you." She smiled through gritted teeth and quickly walked Jamie out of the house.

"What are we doing?" Jamie asked as they stepped out onto the dirt path.

"We have to go find Reid, that's all," she answered, trying to keep her voice level. Jamie stared at her as she walked before shrugging and following her. Annalise wasn't sure where exactly Reid was, but she figured if she could find a ranch hand, she would be able to find him. Her stomach turned at the thought of Laura coming to look for Reid and wanting to talk with him. She almost wanted to be jealous but she just couldn't. Laura had burned down her relationship with Reid and was only now feeling bad about it. There was nothing left for Annalise to be jealous about. Reid has seemed more than over it when they had talked coming home from the cattle auction.

They reached the closest barn and Annalise quickly pulled the door open. "Reid?" she called into the silent building. When nothing returned her call immediately, she pulled the door shut and they quickly walked around the building and towards the next barn. Before they could even reach it, Wade stepped out from where he was working on some barn siding.

"Is everything alright? I heard you yelling for Reid," he said, putting down his tools.

"Everything is fine. Do you know where he is?" Annalise responded. Wade raised an eyebrow at her, not quite seeming to believe her, but he gestured ahead, away from the barn and close to the nearest pasture. "Thank you," she said with a tight smile before turning Jamie and heading in the direction Wade had pointed. Annalise breathed a small sigh of relief when she saw Reid step into view from around his familiar blue-gray colored horse.

Chapter Twenty-Two

Reid was brushing the dirt of Lycan when he heard his name mentioned outside the barn. He patted the horse once and walked out. To his surprise, he saw Annalise marching over, Jamie protectively encircled in the arms as she determinedly made her way to him. He hurried over to the fence and climbed over it, hoping down on the other side and jogging to meet her.

His heart pounded as she approached. He had never seen her so serious before. Her mouth was pulled in a tight line and her face had a ghostly appearance to it. "What happened? Is something wrong?" he asked as they neared him. They reached each other and he had to fold his arms to keep from trying to comfortingly embrace her.

"I um, well," Annalise stammered. Her free hand pulled at the side of her dress and wouldn't stay still. "It's Laura. She arrived at the house," Annalise was finally able to say. Reid blinked in surprise. "I'm sorry for letting her in but she was crying and well, I wasn't sure what to do." Annalise's own eyes seemed to shimmer with unshed emotions.

Reid quickly reassured her, "That's alright. I'll take care of it." His eyes locked with hers, and he looked at her while keeping himself calm, until he could see her visibly relax. After a quick smile at her, he dropped down on one knee to get a better view of her brother, still held tightly by her protective arm. "Would you like to go see some baby cows? There were a few born recently and they are very charming. Wanna meet them?"

"Yes," Jamie exclaimed, nearly jumping up and down in excitement.

Reid ruffled the boy's hair before pointing Annalise in the right direction. "They're in that barn. Make sure to stay out of the stalls though, so the mother cows don't get upset. If you need anything, let Wade know. I should be back soon." Annalise nodded and they slowly headed in that direction. Reid watched them go for just a moment before turning and quickly striding towards the ranch house. He couldn't help but feel angry as he walked.

Why would Laura show up crying and causing problems at his house? She didn't belong here anymore. She wasn't welcome here anymore. He no longer trusted her and therefore, she had to go. His face felt almost on fire and his heart was pounding by the time that he opened the front door. He quickly observed the silent house, his gaze scanning the empty rooms. He walked through, his boots echoing on the floor.

"Reid, is that you?" came Laura's voice from the dining room. Reid found her exactly where she had been left, the cup of tea still in her hands. "Thank heavens," she said when she saw him. New tears began to erupt from her eyes. Reid stood awkwardly on the opposite side of the room, uncertain about what was proper in this situation. Finally, her sniffles came to an end and she looked up at him through red-rimmed eyes. "I wasn't sure if you were going to come talk to me."

"Well, I'm here," he answered, still feeling uncomfortable. He shifted his weight between his feet before he moved forward and stiffly sat down in the seat across the table from hers. "What's going on Laura? Why are you were?"

Her bottom lip pouted out. "I'm just so sorry Reid. I never should have left you for Carter." Her fingers fidgeted with the cup in her hands and she had a hard time meeting his gaze. "Would you ever consider taking me back?" Her question fell into the stiff air of the room and seemed to float uncomfortably between them. Reid shifted in his seat, wishing that he had sent Wade to send her away instead of coming himself. He allowed the silence to linger as he honestly considered her question. If she had come back to him in the days after leaving him, when he was at his lowest and must vulnerable, he would have definitely taken her back. But now? He mulled over how his heart felt and to his surprise he found that he didn't miss Laura at all.

All he could think of now was the way that he felt for Annalise and how much he cared for her. How much he loved her. He had never felt this way about Laura, he realized with surprise. At the time, Reid thought he had felt deeply for Laura, but now he knew that it was only a small, shallow pond compared to the ocean depth of love that he was capable of. Love that had grown for Annalise. "I wish for your happiness," he finally said, his words coming slowly but steadily, "but I have already found someone."

"Can we please at least be friends?" she asked without hesitation.

Reid frowned. While he immediately wanted to tell her 'no', the recent sermon of loving thy neighbor was still circling through his mind. So instead, he nodded yes. He knew it was what Annalise would do. Laura immediately smiled widely at him, clearly happy with his response. He stood up from the table and cleared his throat. "Do you have a ride coming to pick you up or were you planning to walk back to Carter's ranch?" He had seen that there was no horse or wagon hitched up outside.

"Oh," she said, glancing down at the ground. "I was planning to walk back." He frowned once more, knowing that it wasn't very safe for a young woman to walk the paths alone, especially if it started to get dark.

"I'll go hitch up the wagon and get you back to town," he told her gruffly. "Wait here and I'll come back to fetch you when it's ready." He hurried outside.

As he walked over to the barn which held all the cart equipment, he spotted Wade carrying his large tool case, walking away from the barn he had been repairing. "What's going on, boss?" Wade asked, shuffling faster to keep up with Reid.

"Laura needs a ride back to town," Reid answered briefly. Wade frowned but kept any thoughts he had to himself. "Are Annalise and Jamie still doing good?"

"Yes," Wade nodded. "They're still checking on the baby cows. Jamie seems to think they're quite fun. I don't think I've ever heard him laugh so much." Reid smiled at this. "Do you still have that meeting this evening with the new investors and the Williams brothers?"

Reid let out a groan and briefly closed his eyes, his step hitching slightly. "Yes, but I nearly forgot about it. I was planning to ride Lycan there." He frowned. He had been excited to ride his horse to the meeting with the clients and investors for dinner. But now that he was taking the wagon, he would have to use a different horse, as Lycan was often very grumpy about pulling the wagon.

"You should have enough time," Wade said with a shrug.

"That's beside the point," Reid voiced. "Why would she walk here? Because now I have to give her a ride back, it's the right thing to do. But I would rather have used my time differently."

Wade gave his back a large pat while shrugging, not seeming to think it was such a big deal. "Please let Annalise know that I won't be back until late tonight and to not expect me at dinner," Reid finally told him with a sigh. Wade nodded and then the two men parted ways as Wade continued on to work on a different part of the barn and Reid headed in to get a horse and cart ready for the trip into town.

Reid gathered one of the well-mannered brown geldings and got him hitched up to the wagon. Driving him out of the barn, they headed over to the house. He stopped the horse and waited for a moment, expecting that Laura would have been waiting for him. When she didn't appear, he let out a sigh. After a quick climb down to the ground, he headed inside to get her. She was just inside the door, examining some of the wall decorations. "This is lovely," she told him, gesturing to the painting of a stream.

"It's always been there," Reid said, surprised that she didn't remember it.

"Oh, of course," she giggled to herself. She followed him out of the house and graciously accepted his help climbing up and into the wagon.

"Where should I drop you off? At Carter's ranch?" He did his best to not scowl as he asked.

"The general store in town would be perfect, actually," she replied cheerfully.

He gave her a quick nod and then pulled himself up into the seat beside her and with a flick of the reins, they were off and headed to town. Reid found himself extremely grateful that he didn't have to make conversation with her on the way back to town. They rode down the paths and he allowed his mind to be silent as he simply took in the scenery.

When a thought did appear in his mind, it was almost always of Annalise. He wondered what she was doing. If she liked the cattle and if she was thinking of him. The wagon began to get closer to town. He steered the horse to follow the next turn and soon they were on the wide, bumpy town road. They followed the path to the other side of town until they arrived at the general goods store.

He pulled the horse up to the hitching post and then hopped got down. Without bothering to tie up the horse, he crossed to the other side and extended his arm to help Laura down.

"Thank you so much. I look forward to seeing you again," she smiled at him and then turned and headed into the store.

Reid chewed the inside of his lip, not knowing what to make of this change in attitude from Laura. With a shrug, he climbed back up on the wagon and turned his horse to head back toward the nice restaurant where he would be having his meeting. His horse picked its way carefully, clip-clopping down the road. Reid directed him to the hitching post that belonged to the restaurant and stopped there. He was earlier to the meeting than he would have liked, but he knew that was better than being late.

At the cattle auction, he had told Annalise about how successful his ranch had become since nearly losing it all. And while it was true that they were doing well, the only way that they could do better now was to get new customers and hopefully some more land. He was hoping that the Williams brothers would be able to help him secure some more success for his ranch tonight. With a nervous sigh, he climbed down from the wagon and got ready to tackle this new opportunity, a successful outcome on the horizon. But even as he walked into the fine building which should have held his attention completely, he couldn't help but smile as a thought of one day bringing Annalise to dinner her crossed his mind.

Chapter Twenty-Three

Annalise pushed her needle through the fabric, stitching up a hole in the shirt. She sucked in a breath quickly and frowned as the sharp needle poked one of her fingers. Correcting its placement, she continued sewing. She and Jamie were sitting on the couch in the living room. While she worked on mending a small pile of Reid's older shirts that he had begrudgingly asked her to mend, Jamie worked on writing his letters, his fingers pinching the pencil tightly and his eyebrows scrunched together. "Oh, your letter 'S' is backward," Annalise told him.

He let out an exasperated sigh before quickly erasing it and trying again. She felt like letting out a large sigh as well but chose against it, knowing that it wasn't proper for an adult to display their dissatisfaction so. She finished her line of stitching, pulling the string tight and knotting it. Using a pair of scissors, she cut the extra thread. Placing her sewing stuff down, she neatly folded the shirt and set it on her pile of mended clothes.

She grabbed the next item to be mended and her mind wandered as she stitched. Her fingers moved in twitchy motions as her stomach twisted at the thought of Laura talking with Reid. She was his ex-fiancé. Everything was going to be complicated when dealing with relationships like that. Annalise wondered how their talk had gone and if Reid had decided to forgive Laura for what she had done to him. She felt the air get trapped in her chest as she wondered if he might want her back.

Was it possible? Her mind began to spiral at the thought and her fingers stopped moving, her hands no longer working as her mind did flips. If Reid and Laura got back together, what would happen to Jamie and her? Would he send them back? Throw them out? She hadn't even gotten a chance to talk with him about any of it, other than delivering the message that Laura wanted to talk with him.

The previous day, Reid had directed them to the baby cows which her brother had been ecstatic about. He had loved watching the young creatures leap about, flicking their little tails and chasing their mothers around the stalls. It had taken a while to finally convince him to leave the barn, but she needed to get started making dinner, or else everyone would be hungry for the long night. As they left the barn, Annalise had glanced around, trying to see if she could spot Reid or Laura.

When she'd come across Wade and asked him were they might be, he had told her about Reid taking Laura into town and about his meeting there. "He said he'd be late for dinner and not to wait for him."

Throughout the rest of the day, Annalise felt an ache as she missed Reid and wondered if she held any part of his heart like he did for her. She went about her normal business, making dinner, cleaning, and spending time with Jamie, but there was no passion in her actions as she worried about the future and the past, and how they might soon crash into each other.

Why had Reid's former fiancée come to visit in such a state? Why had she calmed down enough to go back to town so soon? What did she want? That night she lay in bed, looking up at the ceiling, unable to rest or even consider sleeping. Her mind held too many unanswered questions. It was a few hours past sundown when she heard the cart pulling up to the ranch. Reid was quiet as he put away the horse, but she heard him coming up the stairs and going into his bedroom. As soon as his door shut gently, she breathed a sigh of relief. He had made it home. She finally allowed herself to relax and fall into a deep sleep.

The next morning, she woke up on time and got Jamie and herself ready for the day. Once downstairs, they started making breakfast. Soon the workers were crammed into the kitchen, getting their plates of food and then dispersing to the table. Wade was last in line and Reid was not with him.

"Will Reid be joining us for breakfast?" she asked.

"He had a meeting with the bank this morning. I think he left for it a few hours ago."

"Oh," she replied with surprise. "He's been gone quite a lot lately."

"He should be back later this afternoon," he assured her, giving her a kind smile. She did her best to return the smile but couldn't help but feel empty inside, even after eating her share of food.

After breakfast was done, she got started on cleaning. Once she had everything wiped down, Annalise put away the last of the clean dishes and then made her way to the living room. Then she started mending the shirts while Jamie came to sit by her, his pencil held tightly as he wrote. After an hour of working, the shirts were complete and Jamie had long since given up on his letters, choosing to select some cards from his toys.

Annalise put the last of the folded shirts down in a pile and then turned to look at her brother. He was sitting on the rug on the floor, eagerly shuffling the deck of cards in his hands. Although he tried his best, they occasionally explode from his fingers and cover the floor. Annalise sat down beside him, quickly spreading out her dress around her, tucking the edges under her legs. "Are you ready?" Jamie asked, his voice quick and excited.

"Go ahead and deal out the decks," she said with a laugh. He began to separate the cards with his tongue sticking out slightly as he concentrated. They had just started into their game of cribbage when they heard shouts coming from outside. They quickly stood, leaving the cards scattered on the floor, and hurried outside to see what all the noise was about.

They stepped onto the dirt path and Annalise's mouth fell open when she saw all the chaos. Cows ran in every direction. Most of the ranch hands were running around on foot. They jumped to get out of the way of the stampede of cattle and others hurried to the barns to collect horses.

"Jamie, stay on the porch. Do not leave it until all the cattle have been put away. I have to go help. Alright?" She leaned down to look him in the eye, waiting until he nodded in understanding. Then she turned and ran into the mess, dodging horses, cows, and people. With squinted eyes, she spotted Wade headed into the barn. Following him, she hurried over to the building.

She found him inside, with his horse nearly all saddled up to go as he pulled the cinch tight and secured it. "What happened? What can I do to help?" she asked.

He shook his head, his hands flying as he secured the tack. "A gate was left open and those silly beasts found it and stampeded out. I've got at least two men hurt, maybe more." He pulled himself up into the saddle. "For every cow that we don't get back, that's more money out of Reid's pocket. Even losing just a few of them could really set us back a lot. I've got to go." He turned the horse and quickly galloped out of the barn and into the mess. Annalise jogged to follow him and when she reached the open door, she looked out at the mess of men who were still scrambling and the cows that were disappearing into the distance.

A lot of the workers were getting on their own horses to chase after the herd. As Wade has said, a few of the men seemed to have some minor injuries from the initial flood of cattle, but no one seemed too hurt. One of the men was leading his horse back towards the barn, limping as he walked. His face contracted with pain at every step. "Are you alright?" Annalise asked, hurrying over to help him. He handed her the reins and leaned back on his good leg with a large intake of breath.

He shook his head, "My leg isn't going to make it. I can't quite get myself up on the horse with just one good leg. And honestly, I'm in too much pain right now to think about chasing after all of them." She glanced with despair from his hurt form out towards the cattle which were now small dots in the distance.

A crazy idea found its way into her mind. "Can I borrow your horse?" Her heart thudded wildly in her chest. She clenched her hands at her side, willing them to stop shaking.

"What for?"

She took a deep breath, "I'm going to help bring the cattle back." She turned and started sizing up the horse, eyeing the stirrup that she would have to get her foot to.

"Do you even know how to ride?" he asked, his voice full of uncertainty.

"I've done it before," she said and lifted her chin. She squared herself up to the horse, grabbing the saddle horn with her left hand and the back of the saddle with her right hand. Jumping higher than she ever had before, she launched herself up and jammed her stomach against the saddle. Her feet scrambled, trying to find the stirrup. Just when she started to slide back down, a sturdy hand grabbed her shoe and slid it into the steady stirrup. She pushed herself up and swung her leg over, seated on the horse, not centered, but on the saddle nevertheless. "Shew," she breathed out. "Thank you for your help."

He shrugged with a small smile on his face. "If you're crazy enough to chase after the cattle, then I guess I'll be crazy enough to help you."

"Thanks," said, still trying to slow her breathing. "Jamie is on the porch. Do you think you could keep an eye on him? It would probably be a good place for you to sit and relax as well."

"Yes ma'am," he nodded to her. She gave the reins a shake and the horse started trotting. The movement made her heart rate spike even more as she worried about falling off and getting injured again. But then she pushed her heels into the sides of the horse and it leaped forward, racing after the cattle. Annalise held on for dear life as they raced across the pastures. Thankfully, the horse seemed to know where it needed to go, and all she had to do was not fall out of the saddle.

Her body bounced uncomfortably and the wind whipped at her eyes, causing them to tear up. Her hair encircled her face and she wondered if the horse was going even faster than the train had. She continued to let the horse lead and it soon approached two of the cows who had stopped to drink water at a little creek.

They looked up at her and her horse as they approached and she wondered briefly if they were going to start running once more. But instead, they huffed and remained still. It occurred to Annalise then that perhaps she was in over her head. She had no idea how to herd the cattle back into the farm. Slowly, she led her horse to walk around the cows so that she stood between them and the rest of their freedom.

"Back to the ranch now," she told them, her voice slightly shaky. "You've been gone for long enough." She nudged her horse to walk closer to them. They stared at her, unfazed. She bit her lip and inched her horse closer by carefully nudging his sides; his nose almost touched the cow. At the increase of closeness, the cow spun away and trotted out of the stream and started heading back towards the ranch, away from her horse. Annalise's mouth fell open in a surprised smile at this. She watched in amazement as the other cow followed its friend. Without waiting for her command, her horse started following the cows, staying right behind them as he had been trained to do so many times before. As they got closer to the ranch, a few other cows joined their group, leaving the long bushes they were chomping to join up with the closest thing to a herd. As they got right up to the ranch land, she realized she had no idea how to get them into the fenced-in pasture. Thankfully, a waving arm caught her eye. Wade was standing at the fence on the other side of the property, ready to open the gate. She managed to turn her horse and he moved around the cattle to turn them toward Wade. They got closer and Wade opened the gate wide. The cows happily entered their area and stopped to munch on more grass.

"Did you herd those five cows all by yourself?" Wade asked while he secured the fence.

"Well, I was there but it was mostly my horse who knew what to do," she said shyly.

He nodded his head in a knowing manner. "Cornskipper."

"What?" she asked, confused.

"The horse you're riding." He pointed to the brown gelding underneath her. "His name is Cornskipper. He's been herding cattle since he was a little thing."

Wade pulled himself back up into his own saddle and started riding away. He glanced back at her. "Are you coming? We've still got more cattle to wrangle."

"Oh, okay. Yes." She tapped her horse's side and they hurried to catch up to Wade. Soon they were cantering back through the fields, heading in a direction that no one else had checked yet. It wasn't long before they found a few more of the loose cattle. As they worked, Wade would yell helpful tips to Annalise and she did her best to adjust to the new words and explanations that were thrown at her. She was mostly thankful for Cornskipper though, who was a far better rancher than she was. When they had caught a total of fifteen cattle between them, they started heading back to the ranch, with the hopes that the hands had found the rest of the cows.

"If there are cows who don't get found, what will happen to them out here?" she asked, looking around at the woods and farmland with uncertainty.

"A farmer might find one and take it, or try to find its owner by the brand on it. If a human doesn't find it, it will have to defend itself from other wild animals like bears, mountain lions, and wolves. But if it can keep itself healthy and away from predators, it will live a happy life, most likely. It would be a big loss of money for us, however, if we aren't able to find them all." They continued the journey and soon the ranch was in sight. "Do you want to open the gate this time?" Wade asked as they got closer to the pasture.

"I'm not sure," Annalise hesitated. "You would probably be better at it. I've never opened the gate before."

"It's easy," he said. "Just ride ahead of us, make sure to give enough space between yourself and the cattle. And then you have to shift the latch to get it to unlock. Pull open the gate wide as we get close, and the cows will go right in."

Annalise's fingers fidgeted nervously but finally, she nodded her head, figuring that this job might be easier than taking care of fifteen cattle by herself. Turning Cornskipper, they skirted around the cattle at a walking speed at first. She quickly realized that they would not be able to make it to the gate first at this rate. She dug her heels into his sides and they sped ahead, soon passing the cows. They ran up to the fence and she pulled Cornskipper to a stop.

After a quick nervous gulp, she swung her leg over his side and dropped to the ground out of the saddle. Her legs nearly gave out under her and she swayed, holding onto Cornskipper's side to keep from falling over. Seeing that the cows were getting close, she awkwardly hobbled over to the fence and fiddled with the latch until she got it to move. She pulled the gate open, jogging to get out of the way just as the cows sped through, spreading out and slowing down once in their pasture. Wade brought up the rear and once it was just him outside of the pasture, Annalise dragged the gate shut. She played with the latch for a moment before it clicked in place and the gate became immobile.

"I've got to tell you, Miss Owens, you sure are turning into a real rancher's wife," Wade said with a smile. Annalise felt her face heat up and she couldn't help but look at the ground, trying to keep a smile off her own face. "Come on, let's head over to the porch, I think I saw the guys waiting there with Jamie."

Annalise went to retrieve Cornskipper, who was waiting patiently for her at the fence. She debated on riding over to the porch or just walking him. Just the thought of climbing back up into the saddle made her legs feel like cramping. She wasn't even sure she would be able to make it up the stairs to her bedroom that night. So, she took his reins and led him over, following Wade to the front of the house.

Just as he'd said, there were six ranch hands sitting on the porch around Jamie, laughing at something that he was saying. Wade dismounted from his horse and tied him to one of the fence posts. Annalise followed his lead and tied Cornskipper to the fencepost as well, giving the horses enough room between each other to be happy.

"He sure does tell the best stories," one of the men said as he saw her approaching. She smiled in response and felt immediately grateful that so many people had stayed to keep an eye on Jamie. She knelt down to where he was sitting and wrapped him in a quick hug before giving his hair a ruffle. As she stood, she noticed someone familiar.

"How are you doing?" she asked, seeing the man who had loaned her Cornskipper. "I'm sorry that I hadn't gotten your name before."

"Nothing a good drink can't manage," he said with a chuckle. "And you can call me Charlie, Ma'am." He was propped up on a chair, his injured leg high in the air. "How did Cornskipper treat you?"

"Truthfully, he did so well on his own that I'm not really sure I was needed at all," she laughed.

Charlie shook his head with a chuckle. "That horse could do it all himself but I do think he enjoys the company." At his statement, some of the other workers let out a chorus of jokes about if Cornskipper truly didn't need Charlie.

"Alright guys, let's settle down," Wade interrupted. "How many was everyone able to recapture? Is there anyone still out and looking?" They began to count through all the workers and how many cattle each person had brought back. After a few extra minutes were spent double-checking their math, Wade turned to everyone with a large smile on his face. "We got 'em all back!"

Whoops and cheers erupted from everyone. Annalise lingered for a moment, enjoying the camaraderie of it all. But then she gestured for Jamie to follow her and they slipped back inside the house and headed to the kitchen to start on the celebratory dinner.

Chapter Twenty-Four

"What do you mean I've been outbid?" Reid asked, doing his best to keep his anger in check. "Just last week I came in here and I talked with you, do you remember that?"

"Yessir, of course," the small, wiry man answered as he peered through his glasses.

"We talked about the piece of land right beside my property that I wanted to buy. We got a contact drawn up and an amount settled on. I told you I would be back this week with the money and then it would be mine. Yet," Reid drew in a breath, trying to maintain his composure, "...you are now telling me that someone has outbid me."

"That is correct, sir," the man answered, fidgeting with the papers in his hands.

Reid brought a closed fist up to his mouth and placed his other hand on the counter in front of him. "Can I counter bid the amount that was placed on the property?"

"I'm sorry, sir, but the selling party already agreed to the buyer's bid. It has been sold and is no longer available."

"Of course. And who purchased the property and outbid my amount?"

"That information is confidential, sir."

Reid nodded slowly before finally grabbing his own paperwork and the large bag of cash that he had brought with him and turned to head out of the solicitor's office. "Thanks for all the help, Mr. Bingham." He left before he could hear the response. Leaving the office behind, he stalked down the street, fuming as he made his way to his wagon. Even though Mr. Bingham hadn't told him who had purchased the land, Reid knew, deep in his bones, that it was Carter who had once again ruined his plans. He let out a deep sigh and tried to refocus his thoughts.

He hadn't needed that land but it sure would have been a great expansion for his ranch. If Carter was willing to spend that much money and effort to take things Reid didn't even need, what would he be willing to do to take away what he really cared about? He stepped down onto the street and walked over to the hitching post to untie the white and brown spotted horse Blossom when he heard a woman calling his name.

"Reid," she called again. He turned to look and saw that it was Laura, hurrying towards him and wobbling slightly in a fancy pair of shoes.

"How are you, Laura? What brings you to town?" he asked politely, even though he wasn't in the mood to talk.

"Oh, well actually I was hoping to find you," she said. "You see, I'm just so grateful that you forgave me for what happened in the past. And I was interested in getting some time to talk with Annalise over a cup of tea. She has just been so kind and forgiving." Laura smiled widely at him.

"She is," he agreed slowly. He wasn't sure how good of an idea it was to bring Laura around and have her spend so much time with Annalise. Their past could be forgiven, but it would still be hard to forget. Yet, as if she was there with him, he could hear her in his head telling him to 'be charitable' to Laura. His hesitation wavered. He considered how there were no other women on the ranch, and maybe it would be a good thing for Annalise to have a friend as she had to be pretty lonely.

"Alright," he agreed. "You can ride back with me to go and talk with Annalise. Do I need to drive you home or will you be alright to walk?"

"I'll walk back home," she agreed quickly. Reid glanced down at her shoes again, wondering at how uncomfortable she would be walking miles in them, but he shrugged to himself. If that's what she wanted to do, he wasn't going to stop her. He helped her into the wagon, untied Blossom, and climbed up next to her. With a quick shake of the reins, they were off and returning to his ranch.

The miles passed steadily as Blossom trotted along. Soon the ranch was in sight, and Reid couldn't have been happier. He'd been away from his land for too long and it was time for him to get back to his livelihood. But, knowing that he had Laura with him, he drove Blossom up to the hitching post closest to the ranch house. Now stopped, he climbed down and tied up Blossom before helping Laura down from the wagon.

Escorting her inside, he held the front door open for her to enter. As they stepped into the house, he could hear noises coming from the kitchen that pointed to Annalise working on dishes. As they moved towards the sounds, he saw Jamie playing with some toys in the living room. He didn't notice them so they kept moving until they got to where Annalise was. The floor creaked under Reid's weight as they reached the doorway. At the sound, Annalise spun around and caught sight of them. Her eyes immediately widened and her mouth opened like she was going to say something, but then it closed just as fast.

"Hey," he said while giving her a large smile. "I'm back from my errands, but Laura wanted to talk with you about yesterday."

Annalise paused, soap and water dripping from her hands to the floor as she looked between them with an expression he couldn't read. "Alright," she finally replied. "Would anyone like some tea or biscuits?"

"That would be lovely," Laura said with a large smile. Laura and Reid headed to the dining room and sat at the table while Annalise got the food and drinks. Laura remained silent, as she had the whole ride over, and didn't offer to help in any way, seeming content to smile vacantly at Reid while Annalise waited on them. Reid about to get up and help Annalise when she appeared in the doorway. He stood and helped to distribute everything as she took a seat.

"I'm so glad that I was able to come talk with you. Speaking with Reid yesterday was just so refreshing and now I don't feel like I'm carrying this heavy weight around." Laura smiled brightly. "I was wondering, however," she began. She turned to Reid as she finished her thought, "Can I speak to Annalise alone, woman to woman? There are some things I want to talk with her about that I just don't think you'll be interested in."

Reid looked over at Annalise and their gazes held for a long moment as he mulled over what he wanted to do. But finally, he nodded. "I'll bring Jamie along with me so that you won't have to worry about him."

"Thank you," she said. Her smile was full of sincerity as their gazes locked. He stood and left the dining room. Retrieving Jamie from the living room, Reid neatly offered something he knew Jamie wouldn't turn down. "Do you want to go check on the baby cows and see how they're doing?" Jamie nodded with great force, a smile brightening his face. They headed toward the front door and once they were outside, they raced each other over to the barn, Jamie excited to see the baby cows, Reid worried about what on earth his ex-fiancée could possibly want to say to his almost wife.

Chapter Twenty-Five

Reid and Jamie disappeared from view as the front door shut behind them. Annalise could just barely make out the sound of them heading to the barn before it was silent once more. She looked up at Laura and they silently stared at each other before Laura finally spoke.

"I know your secret," she said in a low and calm voice, her eyes glinting with the knowledge. "But I'm here to help you."

Annalise felt her blood run cold. Her heart pounded in her chest. What secret was Laura talking about?

"I'm not sure what you're referring to," Annalise said, looking away as she set her teacup on the table.

"*Lilyrose Brothel*-- does that name sound familiar to you?" Laura said it as a question, but they both knew the answer by the way her voice ended almost in a statement. Annalise felt the blood drain from her face as her head spun. But still, she didn't speak, uncertain of how to get out of this situation. Laura nodded, her gaze trained on Annalise.

"I had hoped it wasn't true. But alas, it seems you haven't been as honest and upfront with Reid as he might think." Annalise swallowed the guilt that had been rising in her chest. In their few letter exchanges, Reid had never asked where she lived, only what she did. She had answered honestly about helping clean and take care of a business. She knew that he would think she had been with men if she told him what that business actually was. No one wanted a mail-order bride from a brothel. Before Annalise could even think to deny the claims, Laura calmly pulled out something from her pocket and set it on the table for Annalise to see. It was a letter, still in its envelope, from Lucy, one that Annalise had been patiently waiting for. Her own name was written in clear, easy-to-read letters at the center of the envelope. And the return address, written in the top left corner had been meticulously circled with a pencil. "Carter bribed the mailman for any mail addressed to you. And this letter came from the Lilyrose Brothel," Laura told her with a shrug.

"It's just an address, it could have come from anywhere in that town. The general store, the saloon, the post office itself," Annalise countered, doing her best to sound calm and confident.

Laura shook her head, not fooled by Annalise's explanation. "It didn't take long for Carter to figure out that it belonged to the brothel. He really only had to ask a few people to verify the address and your secret was uncovered."

Annalise leaned forward desperately; her voice quiet but high-pitched. "Please don't tell Reid about this. Jamie and I have nowhere else to go if he decides that he no longer wants us." Fear coursed through her and her mind ran quickly through different scenarios. Having to return to the brothel. Having to live on the street. What were they going to do?

"I'm really sorry," Laura said. "That's why I'm here, to warn you. Carter is desperate to tell Reid the truth. He plans to come over here tomorrow himself to tell Reid. But I want to help you."

"Tomorrow," Annalise repeated, feeling as if the world was coming down around her. "That's not enough time," she whispered as stress coursed through her veins. It took everything in her to not immediately run up the stairs and start packing their bags.

"I want to help you," Laura said again with stronger emphasis. "I'm not going to leave you to deal with them by yourself."

Annalise looked up at her in surprise. "You'll help me?"

Laura let out a sigh. "Carter wants to take anything he can from Reid. Anything and everything. His land, his money… you." They stared at each other for a brief moment, letting the implications settle before Laura continued. "He's offered you a deal. Come work in his kitchen, just as he offered all those weeks ago at the train station. If you do, he won't tell your secret, you will be saved from public disgrace, and Reid will never have to know that you lied to him."

Annalise's stomach twisted in discomfort. "And what about Jamie?"

"Jamie, of course. He would get to stay there as well. He could grow up a normal boy, attend school, and start working when he's older."

"What if I don't agree to the deal?"

"Then your entire life will be destroyed. Who's going to want you two after that?" Laura asked, her eyebrows raised high. "And I know Reid hasn't been paying you anything. You'd have to live on the streets," she whispered, sounding completely horrified at the idea.

Annalise felt her heart clench at the thought and she pinched her lips together to keep from crying. The only way she could guarantee that they wouldn't have to live on the streets was to go with Carter. Yet her heart broke at the thought of leaving behind their life here, with Reid. But Jamie had to come first. He always had to come first. Slowly, she nodded, as tears began to drip from her eyes, no longer able to be contained. "We'll go with you. Tonight, after everyone is asleep and I've had a chance to pack our bags, then we will go."

Laura simply nodded, sipping her tea and acting like that was the only outcome that Annalise could have ever reached. She finished her drink and set her cup down lightly, stood, and collected the unopened letter. "You can have this back once you arrive at Carter's." Her voice was clipped and straightforward, leaving no room to negotiate. Then she took a different slip of paper out of her pocket and quickly scribbled some notes onto it before she slid it across the table to Annalise. "Here are your instructions. Follow them, and you'll be able to breathe easily, knowing the Carter won't expose you." Then she left the room without another word, heading through the house and out the door.

Annalise sat at the table, frozen as the silence settled over her. Then she grabbed the note and quickly read through the instructions for how Laura would receive her that night. Finishing the words, she hid the note in her pocket and hurried over to the front windows to peek outside.

She could just see Laura walking back down the road toward her home. But she did not see Jamie or Reid. Turning from the window, she ran up the stairs and to their room to begin hurriedly packing away their things in their bags. She was nearly done packing when she heard the front door open. The sound startled her and she stuffed the suitcases under the bed and straightened the bedsheets before hurrying down the stairs while forcing her mouth to smile.

"Annalise?" Reid called, just as she came down the stairs. "There you are," he said with an easy smile. "I saw Laura walking back to town. I didn't realize that she would be leaving so quickly."

"Oh, yeah. She just came to talk for a moment." Annalise's voice hitched slightly. "But I think she has other things she has to attend to."

"Of course," Reid agreed.

Annalise leaned down to Jamie. "Did you have fun seeing the baby cows?"

"Yes," he replied, a large smile on his face. "But I think they're already bigger than last time." His voice came out exasperated as he threw up his hands.

Reid and Annalise chuckled at this. "They tend to do that," Reid replied, still laughing. He started to back away from them, "I have some things to take care of, but then I'll be back for dinner." His gaze met Annalise and warmth seemed to flood from his kind features. For a moment she started to open her mouth, to tell him that they were in trouble, that she needed help. But just as soon as the moment arrived, it passed, and Annalise closed her mouth. Reid nodded at her and turned away, heading back outside.

Her breath hitched in her throat at the sight of him leaving, but she allowed him to go. Then she turned to Jamie, barely keeping the tears from her eyes. "What should we make for dinner? I think it should be a really good meal."

"Well, everyone always seems to enjoy your pies," he offered, smiling up to her. She knew that pies were his favorite as well.

She returned the smile. "How many pies should we make?"

"Hm," he mused. "How about three pies?" His grin grew larger on his face.

Annalise let out a chuckle but nodded. "We can do that."

The rest of the afternoon they spent making apple pies. While they were cooking in the oven, Annalies got started on frying and seasoning some beef strips and making a salad. She had just finished plating the food and pulling the pies from the oven when all the men began to file into the kitchen, licking their lips and proclaiming how wonderful everything smelled.

"Three pies!" Wade exclaimed as he entered.

"That was my idea," Jamie cried proudly. All the men chuckled at that. They filled their plates to the edges and found seats at the table. Annalise quickly got Jamie his own serving and set him down. She had started making her own plate when Reid entered the kitchen.

"This all looks very good," he said warmly. She smiled back at him but then turned away, unable to look at him for very long. He grabbed a plate and started adding salad to it. "Did everything go alright with Laura earlier?"

"Yes," she answered, quickly changing the subject. "How was your meeting this morning? And the one last night?"

He let out a sigh. "This morning turned out to be not as successful as I was hoping. But my meeting last night went very well." They continued loading their plates and Annalise finished first. She turned to head to the dining room when Reid held up a hand to stop her. "I haven't gotten a chance to tell you this, but I'm glad that you've become a part of our lives. It's been great for all of us." He gestured toward the men in the other room.

"It has been great for us too," she answered before hurrying past him to the table, blinking rapidly. To her relief, Reid didn't try to talk with her much more than thanking her for the food before heading back outside to feed the animals. She spent the evening scrubbing every dish as well as she could, doing her best to leave the kitchen in the best shape it had ever been. While she finished cleaning, she sent Jamie to collect all his toys and bring everything he owned up to their room.

As darkness overtook the night, she put Jamie to sleep in his bed and finished packing their belongings before sitting on her bed and waiting for the signal that Laura had promised to give. Once Laura arrived, it would be up to Annalise to carry Jamie and their bags down the stairs, out the door, and to the wagon which would take them away from the best part of their lives and into Carter's tight grip. Her heart pounded as she sat and listened. And even as she remained silent, tears poured down her cheeks and soaked the collar of her dress.

Chapter Twenty-Six

Carter sat in the study of his ranch. Only a few candles lit the room, keeping the atmosphere dark as only a bit of moonlight seeped in through the windows. While there were many shelves lining the walls from the floor to the ceiling that were full of books, Carter had never touched any of them.

He had hired a collector to put the set together and ever since they had arrived and been shelved, the only hands that touched them were of his cleaning lady to make sure there was not a speck of dust anywhere. While Carter had a very large desk with a very large chair behind it, tonight he sat in the chair that was closest to the window. It was a large, red, puffy item that Carter often deemed to be the most comfortable chair he owned. He had a drink in his hand that he would occasionally swirl around as he sat and thought and listened for any new noises on the ranch.

Even though it was the middle of the night, he was still perfectly dressed in his pressed pants and shirt, shiny boots, and stiff cowboy hat. While he did his best to always have someone else do his work for him, he never missed an opportunity to be well-dressed. From a very young age, his father had heavily emphasized the importance of appearance, status, and reputation. "You can't be anyone of importance in the world without those three things," he had been told gruffly. Although Carter's mother had passed away after giving birth, he was sure that she too would have agreed with his father's ideals and values. Who wouldn't?

With his father's encouragement, he had left his home on the East Coast and traveled a few states away to Illinois to start up in a new area. With the money and reputation he had received from his father, Carter had carefully looked for a way to become successful with the least amount of effort.

He met an old cattle rancher who was looking for someone to share his own dream with. Carter had done his best to befriend the old man and convinced him to sell his land with the promise that he would still get to help manage things. Once the land was in Carter's name, he happily fired the original owner and started growing the land into a prosperous cattle ranch.

He had his father to make proud, and so he worked hard to become the most successful cattle rancher in the state. However, despite his accomplishments, the townspeople continued to talk about some 'young' rancher who was making a name for himself. A boy who had taken over after his parents died and turned a lost cause of a farm into a great success. Reid Shaw.

So Carter Johnson had turned his focus and fixed it to Reid. The one person who stood in the way of his success. How else could his father be proud of him? He had to be the best to earn that. So he began to make plans. Taking away Laura had been just one of the very first steps. He wasn't going to stop until Reid was out of the way.

The moment that Carter met Annalise at the train station, he knew that he had to find a way to use her against Reid. Stealing Laura away from him had been easy enough and he figured he would be able to do it again, even if the circumstances were different.

Carter sat in his office, shaking his head with a laugh. He thought about how foolish Reid was to bring people into his life that he cared about. The people a man cared about were always his greatest weakness. Carter himself was of the personal opinion that you should never trust the people in your life to care for you. He swirled his drink once more and took a gulp. As he waited, he thought back through the plan that he had enacted.

Just a few hours before, Laura had left with one of his men, taking the covered wagon over to Reid's ranch to pick up Annalise and the boy. Laura had never done something like this before, and had blabbered endlessly to him about how anxious she was about it. But the man he had sent with her was an expert in matters like this. Carter did not have a shred of doubt that they would be successful. A large part of his optimism came from the fact that he had already had so much success buying up the land around Reid's ranch and he hadn't even been detected in the process.

Carter stilled and tilted his head as he heard an approaching sound. Then a smile grew across his face. They had returned home. If he had leaned forward just a bit and turned his head to the side, he would have seen the wagon pass, heading for the other side of the house. But instead, he remained perfectly still except to bring the drink up to his mouth and take a small gulp before he swirled it around some more.

There were some small noises in the house and then he heard the wagon wheels crunch on the dirt once more as it drove around the house and to the barn. Soon a small knock sounded on his study door. Laura stepped in and closed the door gently behind her before making her way to where he was sitting. "Annalise and Jamie are here and settled in," she said after stopping a few feet away from him. He smiled widely at her and took another drink. Before he even had a chance to swirl his drink around, Laura broke the silence. "What are you going to do with her?"

His smile fell and his gaze locked onto his wife as he studied her intently. At first, she met his eyes but then her gaze dropped to the ground and she fidgeted slightly, waiting for his response.

The thought crossed his mind then that perhaps for the first time, her devotion to him was wavering. He frowned at this thought. "I'll do whatever I see fit with her. You and I both know why we're here, and what goal we're working toward. We must do whatever we can to keep Reid weak and distracted so that we can finally destroy him and his ranch."

Laura bit her lip. "Is buying up all the surrounding land not enough? And his cows did get poisoned, you said so yourself."

He gripped his glass tightly and willed his voice to remain quiet and level. "Do you not remember the embarrassment he caused us? The suffering pain of watching his ranch rise up to success and our own failure of not completely destroying him? I have his wife, his money, and his connections, and still, he survives. He continues to harass us with his rising numbers in sales and cattle. With his land expansions and wage increases for his workers. We cannot let this go on." He slammed his glass down on the small table beside his chair and stood up. Laura immediately backed up a few steps, her face turned down toward the ground.

"Will Annalise at least stay here?" she asked quietly.

He took a breath and regained his composure, straightening his shirt and buttoning the cuffs. "A woman of her 'skills' might be a very valuable commodity to the right buyer." Laura looked up, her face pinched in a confused frown. Carter waved his hand, dismissing the topic. Then he stepped forward and wrapped his arm around her, pulling her into a tight hug. "We are so close to the end," he whispered, his gentle words tickling her hair. He leaned back to look into her eyes, his fingers caressing her arm in a calming manner. "Soon we can put all of this behind us and just be the most successful ranch in this state. We've worked too hard to let all of this go. Help me finish what we started."

She bit her lip and was quiet for a moment before she finally nodded. He leaned down and they kissed briefly. They interlocked hands and left the room together, the door closing with a small thud in their wake.

Chapter Twenty-Seven

Reid woke up in his bed and blinked his eyes at the bright light streaming in through his window. He sat up immediately, feeling as if something was wrong. Once out of bed, he quickly pulled on his pants and hurried out of his room, listening closely. To his surprise, he heard nothing. The house was devoid of all sounds. It was then that he realized something else was missing.

The smells. Since Annalise had come into his life, the kitchen always smelled of coffee, food, or both in the mornings. But this morning, there were no smells. He walked across the hallway and knocked gently on her door. Perhaps she had slept in and hadn't started making anything yet. When no one answered, he knocked again and waited impatiently for a response. He leaned against the door, trying to hear if anyone was inside. "Annalise, Jamie, are you in there?"

When no one responded, he turned the doorknob, opening the door just a crack, and peeked in, quickly examining the room. A gasp escaped him and he slammed the door open, stumbled into the room, and looked around in shock. All of their belongings were gone. The room was in the exact state that it had been before the train had arrived carrying the Owens. Clean, neat, and devoid of all life. The only thing that had been left was tucked away by the wardrobe.

He walked over to it and looked closer to see that Annalise had left her walking stick. The only thing that wouldn't have fit in her bag. He left it where it was and turning, he raced down the stairs and into the kitchen. All the dishes were clean and put away, just as Annalise had left them the night before.

He sank to the ground, his hands touching the cold wood as a sense of doom pounded through his chest.

The front door squeaked open and he heard footsteps. "Reid? Are you awake yet?" called Wade's voice. Reid had the habit of being up before the sun, getting many things done before heading inside for breakfast. But today he had slept in.

Reid opened his mouth to call for his friend but no sound came out as he felt his body start to grow numb. The sounds of Wade's footsteps got closer until he stepped into the kitchen and found Reid there. "Are you alright?" he quickly asked, dropping down beside Reid. "What's wrong?"

"She's gone," Reid was able to whisper, sitting back on his heels and turning to look at his friend. "They're both gone."

Wade glanced between the empty kitchen and Reid on the floor. "What do you mean, she's gone? Where did she go?"

Reid shook his head numbly. "I don't know. She must have left in the night." His voice remained low, cracking occasionally throughout his words.

"Did you check her room? Maybe she just slept in, like you did," Wade offered.

"It's empty. All their stuff is gone. It's as if they were never here." He leaned back against the wall, allowing his body to become limp.

"Why did she leave?"

"I don't know," Reid suddenly shouted, feeling anger and despair rip through him. "I don't know anything." His voice cracked into a small sob. Wade watched him for a moment before grabbing underneath his arms and pulling him up to his feet. Reid swayed uneasily but did his best to stand. He worried that if he wasn't able to stand on his own, Wade would allow him to drop back to the floor without resistance. He grabbed the edge of the counter and was able to stay on his feet, although his legs shook underneath him.

"You have to pull yourself together," Wade told him in an even tone. "Now use that brain of yours. Why would she leave? Was it her own decision or did something else happen that we're missing?"

Reid ran a hand through his messy hair, trying to get his mind to work. What had occurred the day before? He had the meeting and wasn't able to secure the land, and then... Laura. "I brought Laura back here. She flagged me down in town and wanted to speak with Annalise and thank her."

"Were you there the entire time they talked?" Wade asked.

Reid shook his head, "No, I took Jamie on a walk so that they could talk. And then Laura was leaving soon after that... Could this really have something to do with Laura and Carter?"

"I would bet all the money in my possession that Carter is the reason behind this." Wade folded his arms across his chest.

"He's a nasty person, but why, why would he do this?" Reid asked as he shook his head, not wanting to believe what was happening.

Wade's mouth fell open. "Are you forgetting everything? He stole Laura from you and convinced her to take a deed for your land, money, and important paperwork. He's poisoned cattle and bought up surrounding land. What would stop him from taking Annalise away too?"

"But why would she go with him? Why would she leave? That's what I don't understand," Reid said as he started to walk in circles around the kitchen.

"The *why* doesn't matter. What matters is that you do something about it. You've never done anything before when it came to him messing with what is yours. But you have to do something now. You can't let this one go," Wade said, his voice full of emotion.

As the words hit him, Reid squared his chest and charged out of the kitchen. He ran up to his room, grabbed his shirt, hat, belt, and boots, and quickly pulled them on as he raced down the stairs and outside. By the time he made it to the barn, he was fully dressed. He threw a saddle onto Lycan and jumped on. They raced across the pastures and down the lane, heading straight to the Johnson ranch.

Due to Carter buying up so much property, it didn't take long before Reid was on Johnson land, but he knew that the main house was miles into the property. Rather than taking the roads, Reid ran Lycan through the fields, picking out the safest and quickest way to the main house. A lather was becoming evident on Lycan's neck and rump the closer they got to the house. But soon it was in view, and Reid slowed their pace, allowing his horse to catch his breath.

The large white house was very grand in its construction. Carter had spared no expense. There were many large columns across the front of the house, holding up a balcony on the third floor. Windows lined all sides of the house and there were intricate bushes around the yard. Reid had only been to this house twice before, and he had no desire to visit it again and had even vowed to never return, but he had to make sure that Annalise was alright.

He pulled Lycan to a stop right at the front steps of the house. Immediately, a worker in a clean, black uniform hurried out of the house, offering to take the reins. "You may watch him but do not touch him," Reid told the worker as he slid off the horse. He had trained Lycan to not need to be tied up every moment that he was away, and he trusted his horse to follow his training. "I'll be right back," he said to his mount before patting his neck and running up the stairs to the door. The worker quickly chased after him as Reid slammed the doors to the building open.

"You must wait to enter, sir," the worker yelled after him. But Reid didn't care and he hurried inside, looking around to find no one there at all. Just past the main entryway, the room opened up into a wide circle of space when a large staircase when up the side of the room to where a balcony overlooked the entire floor.

"Mr. Shaw, what brings you to my humble home?" came Carter's voice. "It is always a pleasure to see you." He let out a sarcastic chuckle.

Reid gritted his teeth and looked around the lavishly decorated room before looking up at where Carter stood on the balcony, looking down at him. Carter turned and, incredibly slowly, began to make his way down the stairs. Reid kept his lips pinched together and did his best to avoid glancing at the large paintings, marble statues, and engraved wall molding that surrounded him, a reminder of the wealth this man had and wielded like a weapon.

Instead, he glared at Carter, watching him saunter his way down the stairs. Reid couldn't help but notice that Carter's outfit was just like his home, gaudy and way to fancy to be usable. His entire outfit was white. White pants, jacket, hat, and boots, like a ridiculously clean, matching set. No one would ever help run a ranch with that outfit on. Reid was sure that within the first minute of hard work, it would be ruined.

"I need to speak with Laura," Reid finally said as Carter neared him. As if summoned by her name, Laura appeared on the stairs and looked down at them. Reid noted that she wore a dark gray dress that contrasted vividly with Carter's white outfit.

Carter also noticed that Laura had appeared. He turned to Reid, his eyes narrowing. "It is time for you to go home." Two man-servants stepped out from the side hallways and strode toward Reid, ready to remove him from the house.

Ignoring them, he looked up at Laura. "Annalise is missing. I'll do anything in the world to get her back. Please, do you know where she's gone?."

The servants grabbed his arms and started to pull him back toward the door. He didn't allow himself to be taken easily but he also didn't fight against them. Instead, he continued to stare at Laura, willing her to answer him. But all she did was frown, sadness crossing her features. "I'll do anything," he whispered right before they pushed him out the door. He landed hard on his back and rolled down the first few steps. In pain, he pulled himself up to his feet and looked back at the house in longing. What was he going to do now? He limped down the stairs to where Lycan was waiting for him, munching on some grass right beside the house.

He pulled himself into the saddle and sat for a moment, trying to think of a new plan. He felt foolish that the extent of his previous plan had been to storm Carter's home, asking for her. He had hoped that she would appear, and he could have explained himself to her and begged her to come back. If something needed to be changed at his ranch to make her happier, he would gladly do it. But she hadn't appeared and he hadn't seen any sign of her. It was as if she had completely vanished, and there was nothing he could do about it.

With a sigh, he turned Lycan away from Carter's house and headed toward town. Reid's mind wove through different possibilities before he settled on checking the train station first. Perhaps her being missing had nothing to do with Carter. Maybe she had just been homesick, that was always a possibility.

He urged Lycan into a canter and they hurried to town, Lycan's long legs eating up the distance. As they reached the outskirts of town, Reid slowed down, not wanting to startle anyone and wanting to allow Lycan some rest. If Annalise was anywhere in town, he would have to find her somehow. They went to the train station and Reid left Lycan at the hitching post. He walked quickly up to the ticket booth.

"Mr. Hadler, have there been any trains to Springfield today?" Reid asked.

"Good afternoon, Mr. Shaw. There have been a few. But there will be some more tomorrow if you'd like a ticket for any of them," Mr. Hadler told him.

Reid shook his head. "I'm looking for Annalise Owens. Do you know if she purchased any train tickets today?"

Mr. Hadler shook his head. "I haven't had anyone by that name today."

With a frown, Reid rubbed at his beard. "I don't think she would have used a different name," he mumbled to himself.

"Let me put it this way, sir," Mr. Hadler interrupted him. "I haven't had any women purchase tickets today. Women have been on and off the platform for every train, but only men have made purchases."

"Thank you," Reid told him before grabbing his hand and shaking it quickly. He turned and hurried off the platform, back down to where Lycan was hitched. As he walked, the sounds of bells ringing interrupted his thoughts. Of course, the church. That would be the next place that he would check. He reached Lycan and quickly untied him and mounted. He steered him around and they headed down the street to the church. The building quickly came into view. Reid tied Lycan at the empty hitching post and hurried inside, hoping that Annalise and Jamie would be inside. To his disappointment, as he entered the large room, he found only Pastor Thomas lighting candles at the altar.

Reid hurried down the row to the altar. Pastor Thomas turned to look when he heard Reid's footsteps. "Mr. Shaw, is there anything I can help you with?" he asked.

"Has Annalise come by at all today?" he asked, trying to keep his voice calm.

"She has not," the pastor said, shaking his head. "Is there anything I can do for you or her?"

A rough sigh sounded from Reid's chest. "I guess if she comes by, tell her to stay put. I won't be able to find her if she doesn't stay in one place." He opened and closed his fist in rapid succession, feeling the stress start to overwhelm him.

"Son, I'm not sure what's going on right now, but I think there's a verse you need to hear," Pastor Thomas said, looking at Reid with pity and kindness in his eyes.

"What verse is that, Pastor?" Reid asked.

"Proverbs 3:5-6. 'Trust in the Lord with all thine heart; and lean not unto thine own understanding. In all thy ways acknowledge Him, and He shall direct thy paths.' Whatever's going on, He is already by your side in this."

Reid took a deep breath, trying to calm himself. He wasn't sure that trusting God was the answer to this problem, and yet he didn't know what else to do. He did know what Annalise would want him to say.

"I will try," he finally told Pastor Thomas. The pastor nodded and then Reid left the building, getting back on Lycan. He spent another hour in town, going to every business and building to see if Annalise had come by. To his disappointment, no one had seen her. So, as exhaustion and worry started to overtake him, he turned Lycan to head back to the ranch. His stomach growled at him as they slowly made their way home. The sun would be setting within the next few hours and then this day would be over. His first day without Annalise and Jamie. His heart ached in his chest at the thought of her being gone. He had no idea where to find her. Would she ever return home? As the final miles seeped away, Reid closed his eyes and gave himself a moment, trying to be with God. "I need to trust You. To follow You and know that You will take care of Annalise. Please bring her back to me." He spoke out into the open air. "Please bring her back home."

Chapter Twenty-Eight

The night that Laura came to get them, Annalise had carried Jamie and their bags down the dirt path. After walking slowly, encumbered by her large load, Laura had offered to help carry some of the bags. They made their way down the path, walking in the moonlight until Annalise could see a covered wagon ahead. They loaded the luggage and Annalise climbed into the wagon with Jamie still fast asleep in her arms.

To her surprise, Laura sat with the driver and didn't speak another word to her. She kept her thoughts to herself though, and didn't ask questions as she didn't want Carter to go back on their deal. They rode swiftly through the night. Annalise tried to keep track of where exactly they were going, but the darkness was too much and seemed to fill up the world completely. She remembered the night not so long ago when she and Reid had ridden home on the wagon while darkness was filling the sky. There had been so much life all around her, even in the dark. But now, she couldn't see anything.

There were no lightning bugs, no birds, no crickets chirping. She thought about Reid, sleeping in his bed. What would happen when he woke up? Would he be upset that they were gone? She hoped that he would miss them, but at the same time, she hoped that he would let them go. She had been foolish to think that once she left the brothel, it would never cause her problems again.

"Lord, please watch over Jamie," she whispered into the night. The sound of the wagon wheels on the path overpowered the sound of her words. She slowly ran her fingers along Jamie's hair as she felt her heart clench. "I don't know what's going to happen, but I'm scared. Please keep him safe. Amen." She leaned down to kiss her brother's head.

She took a breath and tried to ready herself for any problems she was going to have to face. Squinting her eyes, she stared out into the night, trying to be aware and observant of anything that might be important. Within just a few minutes, the wagon turned off the main path and headed down a new road that seemed to be well taken care of. The wagon didn't bounce as much and the sounds of the wheels was more suppressed.

When they arrived at their destination, the wagon pulled to a stop, and Annalise climbed out, still holding Jamie. Laura hurried them through the back servant's entrance of a house and up a few flights of stairs. They finally arrived at a room and were ushered in, the bags thrown in with them. Without a single word, Laura pulled the door shut and Annalise heard the key turning and the latch locking. As silence surrounded her, fear began to seep into her body.

The room was dark, with no light coming in except from the keyhole in the door. She walked forward with Jamie still in her arms. After just three steps, her shin smacked into a bed. Placing him down gently, she felt around the bed to find that it was incredibly small and Jamie took up nearly the entire thing. With her arms out ahead of her, Annalise made her way around the room until she had a mental image of their space.

It was an incredibly tiny room that held only the small bed and a chamber pot. Their suitcases took up a large amount of space in the area where they had been thrown. She took a deep breath, willing her heart to calm and her mind to find rest. She just had to get through this night. Tomorrow would be better once she got settled into her new job and made sure that Jamie was doing well. She was sure that things would get better from there.

Annalise walked the two steps over to the bed and did her best to position herself beside Jamie, but she ended up having to fully hug him in order to fit beside him. While the bed was not uncomfortable, it took Annalise a few hours of waiting before her eyes burned strong enough and her head felt fuzzy enough that sleep finally took her over, and she passed out due to exhaustion.

The next time she opened her eyes, the room was no brighter, although a small bit of daylight came through the keyhole in a single beam. She realized that Jamie was awake and holding her tightly, seeming to be afraid. "It's alright, Jamie," she mumbled while she rubbed his back and smoothed down his hair.

"Where are we?" he asked, his voice shocked.

"We had to come to a new place to live," Annalise responded, trying to sound optimistic.

"Where's Reid at?" His bottom lip stuck out.

"He had to stay at his home. I don't think we will be seeing him much anymore," she tried to explain.

"What about the baby cows?" he asked in a hushed tone.

"I'm not sure we'll see them much either," she admitted.

Her brother started crying, tears flooding down his cheeks. "I didn't even get to say goodbye."

"I know, I know," Annalise repeated, trying to soothe him. "There wasn't enough time. But if we see any of them again, I promise I will let you say goodbye." A small grin formed on his face at that thought. He hugged Annalise briefly before rubbing his nose with his shirt and wiping away some snot and tears that had escaped.

She climbed up and out of the bed and went over to the door, hoping that she would be permitted to leave and get ready to work for Carter. As she reached the doorknob, she attempted to turn it and push it open but it was still locked. Fear started to drown her intrusive thoughts grew in number and probability. She felt around for just a moment before finding the chamber pot. "Jamie, when you need to use the restroom, use this instead."

"I can't go to the outhouse?"

"Not right now, you can't. But that's alright," she said, trying to fill her voice with cheer. "Why don't you get out a game for us to play? Your bag is right here." She grabbed it and handed it to him.

"It's kind of dark in here though," he said, clearly not loving the idea.

"That will make it more fun. Trust me. Now what do you want to play?" Jamie worked to get out several items for them to play with. They started with his toy soldiers first before making their way to his drawing materials.

They were nearly through their drawing of a mama and baby cow when Annalise heard someone approach the door. She hopped off the bed quickly as a key was slid into the keyhole. The door opened long enough for someone to shove a tray full of food into the room and then close the door, locking it from the outside once again.

"Excuse me," she called to the person as she tried to pull the door open. "When can we be let out of here? This is not what I was told would happen." To her disappointment, the person did not respond and the sound of footsteps grew fainter.

"Why are we stuck in here?" Jamie asked, his little voice sounding so lost.

"I'm not sure," Annalise admitted. "But we are going to figure it out together, okay?" He nodded his head and they sat huddled together on the bed, eating the bread and cheese and drinking the water that had been provided to them. They spent the rest of the day just the same. Jamie complained every time he had to use the chamber pot, having gotten used to the freedom of the outhouse compared to how they'd managed in the city, but he adjusted well, not even complaining as the room smelt worse with every hour. Bread, cheese, and water were all they had been provided. To Annalise's relief, she convinced Jamie to eat nearly all of it. As the room began to darken even more than it had all day, she assumed that the sun was going down and it would soon be very dark once more.

"Can you tell me a story about Mom?" he whispered.

She held him tighter. "Which story do you want to hear?" she asked.

He shrugged. "A new one. Was she ever stuck in a dark room before?"

Annalise rubbed her face, trying to retrieve memories of the stories her mother used to tell her. "There was a time that Mother was trapped. Not in a dark room, but she was also locked up in a way that she wasn't able to escape. At night, she would always make time to stare at the stars outside. She used to say that the stars helped her see that this was all a part of God's plan. They helped her to keep her trust in Him."

"I can't see the stars here, there are no windows," he said, frowning.

"That's true, but we can imagine them up above us, high in the sky. Their patterns of white lights and magnificence in the black sky."

"I'd rather see them myself."

"Me too," she agreed.

"Are His plans always good?" Jamie asked sleepily.

She paused for a moment, trying to find the right answer. "They might not always seem good at the time," she finally admitted. "Mother was trapped and that might not have seemed good, but if she hadn't been trapped, she would have never had me or you. And you are very good." She squeezed him tighter.

"Did Mother ever escape? I hope so."

Annalise felt her heart break a little as she said, "She did escape, although not in the way that she planned."

"Will we escape?" he asked.

"I don't know God's plan, but I think we can trust that it is good."

"Will Reid help us?"

"I'm not sure,"

"I hope so," Jamie said as he drifted off to sleep.

"I hope so too," she whispered. Her brother became silent and unmoving. She sat and waited patiently, rubbing his back lightly. Soon a small snore came from him. She smiled at this and then climbed out of the bed carefully. She walked over to the door and tried it once more, finding that it was still locked and unmoving. Making her way around the room, she felt along the walls and floor, hoping that she had missed something the night before. With no windows and no candles, the room hadn't brightened up enough during the day to make out too many details.

Her hands trailed along the wooden boards until she felt the stickiness of a spiderweb. She pulled her hand back, shaking it to try and free it from the web. When she couldn't feel the stickiness any longer, she looked closely and could see parts of the web shining as light found it, or perhaps it was her mind inventing something for her to do. She dug through her suitcase until her fingers brushed against the paper and pencil she used for letter writing, and she sat in the darkness for a long while, trying to sketch a spider she couldn't see.

After half an hour of loose sketching and blind guessing, Annalise turned the paper over and hovered the pencil over the blank side, as if she were about to write a letter. Then her hand fell into her lap and she composed a letter in her head, a letter she didn't know if she would ever have a chance to write.

Dear Reid, I'm sorry for not saying goodbye. I never intended for things to end this way. Truly, I thought I would get to spend the rest of my life with you. Maybe not as your wife, but as your friend and housekeeper at least. Since meeting you on the train station platform, I have grown to care for you in ways that I could have never imagined. I always wanted to be in a position where I didn't have to rely on someone else, but now I see that it's not as bad as I was thinking.

Relying on you has become one of the greatest privileges of my life. I wish that I could count on you to save me now, but I believe that I've gotten myself into too much trouble this time. I made this decision because I thought it would be best for Jamie and me, but now I see that perhaps it was the worst decision I could have made. I'm not sure if you will ever read or receive this, but if you do, please know that you have become incredibly valuable to me and I'm so glad that I got to spend those weeks with you. Yours Truly, Annalise.

Tired, she tucked the paper and pencil back into her bag and did her best to climb into the bed with her brother. Weariness began to seep into her and she wondered how long they would be kept as prisoners. This is not the deal she had agreed to. But she did her best to breathe deeply and not alert Jamie that something was amiss, even though something was indeed very wrong.

Only when the room turned completely black did she allow her exhaustion to carry her mind off to sleep. She was deep in a dream when there was a gentle knock on the door. She sat up as the door was being unlocked. The door pushed open and in stepped Laura. Laura squinted her eyes over the small candle in her hand, looking into the darkness. She glanced behind her, studying the hallway before slowly walking forward into the room.

"Laura?" Annalise finally spoke her name. Despite Laura being the reason that they were in this mess, she couldn't help but feel relieved at her presence.

"I'm getting you two out of here," she whispered back urgently.

"What's going on? Why have we been locked in here?" Annalise asked, trying to not wake up Jamie or whoever Laura was worried about.

"Get ready to leave tonight; I have to get you two away from Carter." With those words, Laura closed the door behind her, the lock slipping back into the place and the key shifting in its hole.

Annalise's heart pounded in her chest with such ferocity that she thought it might just explode right out of her body. She held her hand to her chest and sat quietly, trying to understand what had occurred. Laura had told her they would leave 'tonight' but was it not already night? What time was it?

A thick cloud of worry threatened her mind. It was one thing to be locked up with no information. But to be locked up while feeling threatened by Carter? Annalise shuddered and hugged her arms around herself, feeling completely alone. Slowly, she climbed off the bed and maneuvered around the room until she was closest to the door where there was the most space. Carefully, she got down on her knees and began to pray. Her prayers started out small, asking for help with her fear.

Help with their safety. For Laura to be successful in rescuing them. She continued praying for a long time, longer than she could keep track of until she felt herself giving into her exhaustion and allowing her head to rest on her hands. Time passed with her like that, her mind drifting between sleep and prayers.

Thoughts and memories combined with dreams. Then a sound, like a click, woke her up. She looked up through bleary eyes, trying to blink and clear her vision. Had Laura returned for them? Then just as she recognized that someone was approaching her, a bag was thrown over her head and strong arms locked her in place as the person dragged her out of the room.

As she was pulled out, she heard other muffled sounds and then Jamie's scream. They were taking him as well. "Let us go!" she cried out, trying to wriggle out of the hands that held her. But it was no use; they were too strong and didn't care. They squeezed against her until she felt lightheaded, her hot breath filling up the bag, and darkness entered her mind.

Chapter Twenty-Nine

Reid's boots slapped against the worn wooden floor as he paced the length of his small cabin, his fists clenched at his sides. The silence was suffocating and oppressive. Every sound, from the creak of the floorboards to the occasional rustle of the wind outside, seemed louder than it should have.

The house was dimly lit, the low light flickering from the lone table lamp in the corner, casting long shadows on the walls. He wasn't sure how long he'd been at it—minutes, hours, it all blended. He couldn't stop thinking about Carter. Annalise couldn't have left without help, and something about Carter's reaction to Reid bursting into his home combined with Laura's visit the other day told him he had a hand in her disappearance. He'd taken the woman he loved once—what was to stop him from doing it again?

The silence inside the house was too thick as Reid's mind whirred with all the possibilities to find Annalise and Jamie. He could bang on every door in town, ride the train all the way down the line, go the address Annalise had sent her original letters from, break down Carter's door with Wade and a gun at his side. But even if he managed to find her, would she want to come back with him?

Suddenly, the door slammed open. Laura burst into the house without knocking, her face pale and her breathing erratic. The door slammed against the frame behind her as she entered, and she stood there for a moment, clutching the doorframe as if it were the only thing keeping her upright. Reid's heart leaped into his throat as he saw the raw fear in her eyes. She was shaking, and her disheveled appearance made it clear that something was terribly wrong.

"Laura?" Reid's voice came out low, filled with concern. He pushed himself off the wall where he had been standing and moved toward her. "What's going on? What's happened?"

She opened her mouth to speak, but no words came at first. Instead, she collapsed into the nearest chair, her breath coming in shallow gasps. Reid crouched in front of her, trying to steady her, his hand on her arm. Her trembling form seemed so fragile, like a small bird caught in a storm.

"Reid," she finally managed, her voice barely a whisper. "I— I didn't mean to hurt anyone. I didn't know. I thought he was just going to use Annalise... but now..." Her voice faltered as she swallowed hard, her hands trembling in her lap. "He's taken them. He's taken Annalise and Jamie."

Reid's heart seemed to stop beating for a moment. His grip on her arm tightened. "What are you talking about?"

"Carter," Laura's voice broke, and she looked up at him with wide, frightened eyes. "He's taken Annalise and Jamie. He's..." Her breath hitched, and she seemed to fight to control the rising panic in her chest. "Reid, I didn't know. I thought he only wanted Annalise to pressure you, to make you sell him part of your land. But now... now I'm afraid of what he's going to do."

Reid's mind spun, the words not quite fitting together. In the corner of his eye he saw Wade appear in the doorway. He stopped and looked between them, an unspoken question on his face.

"Laura," Reid said, his voice low and steady, though inside, he felt as though everything was falling apart. "What's he planning to do with Annalise?"

Laura's face was pale as she finally looked him in the eye, her tears threatening to spill. "He's going to sell her, Reid. I'm sure of it. He said something about finding a use for her. I didn't believe he meant it, I swear! But when I realized he wasn't going to help like he promised, I was going to let them go. But when I went back they were already gone, and so was he."

She paused, trembling as if the weight of her words was too much for her to bear. "I didn't want to believe it, but now, I know... it's worse than I thought. He's going to sell her to the highest bidder."

Reid stood abruptly, his heart racing as the room seemed to close in around him. His body felt cold, and his mind was flooded with images of Annalise's kind face and Jamie's trusting smile, both of them now caught in the hands of a monster. Carter's betrayal wasn't just about business anymore; it was something far darker, far more sinister.

Reid's stomach turned. "You have to be mistaken," he said, though his voice was unsteady. "Carter wouldn't do that. He's... he's not like that. He wouldn't sell an innocent woman."

Laura looked away as he said the word 'innocent', as if she knew something she didn't want to tell him. But how could anything be worse than what she'd admitted already?

She shook her head, her eyes filled with a pain that struck Reid to his core. "I wish I was wrong, Reid. But I'm not. I've seen the way he looks at her—like she's a commodity, something he can trade or sell. He never cared about her, about me, or anyone else. He only cared about his own plans, his own ambitions." She paused, her voice cracking. "I should have stopped it. I should have told you sooner. But I didn't understand what I was seeing. I didn't think he would go this far."

Reid's hands curled into fists, his jaw tight with anger and frustration The shock of what Laura was saying slowly seeping through him, but a fierce protectiveness began to rise within him, too. Annalise and Jamie had been taken. They were in danger, and he had to find them. He couldn't let Carter win. He couldn't let him hurt them.

"Where are they now?" Reid demanded, his voice sharp as a blade.

She shook her head, hands twisting desperately in her lap. "I don't know. He took them away today without telling me. I don't know if he's already found a buyer—"

He cut her off in disgust. "Stop! Tell me where he is and I'll make him tell me where they are."

"I—I don't know," Laura stammered, her voice trembling. "He doesn't tell me everything. I thought he did, I thought I could trust him, that he loved me. . But he's dangerous. I—" She broke off, looking away, guilt flooding her features. "I never thought he would go this far. I never thought he would hurt her."

"We're going to find them," Reid said with grim determination. He turned to Wade, who was still standing silently by the door, watching the exchange. Wade's gaze had been hard throughout these revelations, his expression unreadable, but Reid knew that his friend was as committed to finding Annalise and Jamie as he was.

"I know," Wade replied, "but we need a plan. Carter's not just going to sit still while we search. We have to be careful."

Reid nodded, his mind moving at a pace faster than he could keep up with. They didn't have the luxury of time, but he knew Wade was right. They couldn't just rush in blindly. They needed to think—strategize.

Turning back to Laura, Reid grabbed her hands and forced her to look him in the eyes. "What did you hear him say about taking her? Who was he talking to?"

Her hands shook in his. "He took the cart and left with them before I could get to them, that's all I know."

"What direction did the cart go?"

"I..." She shook her head helplessly, tears streaking her dust stained face. "If I knew I would have told you."

He looked to Wade. "Someone at that house knows." Wade nodded in agreement and turned, already knowing what needed to be done. Reid looked down at the woman he once thought he would marry, now a shaking, teary mess because of what her new husband had done. To him, to her, to Annalise and her brother. His jaw tightened. "Stay here," he said. "If they come back here before we do, help them."

She stood shakily, wiping tears away. "I could help, I can try to find out more..."

"No. It'll be better if you're not around for the next part."

As he turned to leave, Wade hurried up to the house with two horses saddled. The cold night air hit Reid like a slap to the face as he stepped outside, but it didn't matter. His mind was set. He would find Annalise. He would find Jamie. And whatever it took, he'd bring them both home, safe and sound. He leapt onto his horse and spurred him forward, galloping towards Carter's house. The clock was ticking, but he wasn't about to lose the people he loved. Not now. Not ever.

Chapter Thirty

The world around Annalise was nothing but a blur. The edges of her vision darkened as she tried to force herself to focus, but the weight of the sack over her head, the suffocating pressure against her chest, and the tight grip on her arms made it impossible to think clearly. As her breath came in ragged gasps, she tried to clear her mind, to push through the terror that clawed at her insides, but the darkness was growing, and soon her body gave in.

When she finally came to, the sensation of cool night air around her was the first thing she noticed. The muffled sounds of the world around her began to make sense—there was movement beneath her, the steady creak of wheels turning, and the rhythmic clop of hooves.

She was lying down, her back pressed against a hard surface, and when she tried to shift, she felt the rough edges of a straw-filled sack beneath her. The sack was still heavy on her face. She could hear Jamie's soft whimpers nearby, and instinctively, her body moved toward the sound, trying to reach him despite the pain in her limbs.

"Jamie," she whispered urgently, her voice hoarse. "Jamie, can you hear me?"

Her heart pounded in her chest as she tried to shift again, only to find her wrists bound tightly. She tugged at the ropes in vain, but they were too strong. The memory of being pulled from the safety of her home, of Jamie's scream echoing in her ears as they dragged him away, sent a fresh wave of fear surging through her veins. She squeezed her eyes shut, trying to block out the horror of it all.

"Jamie," she murmured again, this time louder, trying to calm him. "It's going to be alright, sweetheart. I'm here."

She heard the faint sound of Jamie sniffling beside her, followed by a weak, trembling voice. "I'm scared."

"I know, sweetheart. I know. But we're going to be okay. I promise." Her voice cracked with the force of the emotion choking her throat. She pressed her head against his, trying to offer comfort, though she had little to give.

The cart jolted as it hit a bump in the road, and Annalise had to bite back a groan of discomfort. The motion was unsettling, and the cold wind that whipped past them only deepened the fear in her chest. She tried to adjust her position to shield Jamie as much as she could, holding him close with the little strength she had left.

The voices above her reached her ears, low and casual like they were discussing nothing more than the weather or business dealings. But the words they spoke sent a chill down Annalise's spine.

"No, it won't take long," a voice said, one that sounded familiar—cold, smooth. *Carter.* "A woman like her? I'll sell her quick, and for a good price. Don't even bother hitching the wagon."

Annalise's heart stopped. She stiffened, her blood running cold. A brothel. They were taking her to a brothel. Her worst fear was coming true.

"You want me to hold on to the kid while you deal with her?"

"Just make sure he doesn't roll out and start screaming. We'll have plenty of that to deal with when we get him to the workhouse."

Annalise pressed her lips together, holding back the wave of nausea that threatened to overtake her. She'd done so much and come so far to escape this life, to save herself and Jamie from being forced into lives of servitude, and now she was facing the terrifying prospect of being sold back into that hellish world. The thought made her stomach twist painfully, but she didn't let it show. Instead, she began to pray.

"Lord, please," she murmured softly. "Please keep us safe. Help us find a way out of this. I trust in You, even when I cannot see the path ahead."

A soft sob escaped Jamie, and Annalise's heart shattered. She pressed her cheek to his hair, trying to soothe him through the rough sackcloth. "Jamie, it's alright. It *will* be alright, I promise. I'm here."

The driver said something low and dark that made Carter laugh, and Annalise could feel her blood simmering with a quiet fury. She had never felt so helpless in her life, so powerless. The feeling of being at the mercy of men like Carter—men who saw her as nothing more than a piece of meat to be sold and used—was suffocating.

But she refused to break. She couldn't let herself give in to the fear that threatened to drown her. She had to hold on to the strength that God had given her. And she had to keep Jamie safe, no matter what it took.

"Jamie," she whispered again, her voice soft but firm. "I need you to be brave, okay? Just a little longer, and we'll be out of here."

His tiny body trembled in her arms, but he didn't argue. She could hear the catch in his breath as he tried to calm himself.

"I'm scared, Annalise."

"I know, sweetheart. I know." Annalise fought to keep the quiver from her voice. "But remember what we've been taught. God is with us. And as long as we trust in Him, He will lead us through this. He will help us."

She took a deep breath, feeling the wind press against her as the cart continued to rattle over the uneven road. Her throat ached with the weight of her fear, but she swallowed it down. She would not let despair take her. Not now.

The rickety cart jolted again, more violently this time, and Annalise was thrown sideways, her body slamming into the rough wooden side with a painful crack. The air rushed out of her lungs, and for a moment, she struggled to catch her breath, her head spinning. Her heart pounded in her chest as she pushed through the haze of dizziness.

"Jamie!" she gasped, frantic now, reaching for him. Her hands, still bound behind her back, were useless, but she felt the sudden shift in the air around her, felt the absence of his warmth next to her. She turned her head frantically.

"Jamie?" she cried again, her voice sharp with panic. The cart had picked up speed and she could hear raised voices shouting around them. "Jamie, are you okay?"

The sound of Jamie's voice, small and trembling, came from behind her. "I-I'm fine."

Relief flooded through her like a balm, but it was short-lived. The chaos around her was escalating. She heard shouts, the sound of hooves scrambling on the ground, a gunshot, and a yelp of pain. *Bandits*, she thought, the word making her heart race and her hands shake. If the bandits found a woman and child bound in the back of a cart, God only knew what they would do. But maybe, if the fight continued...

She didn't have much time.

Shaking with both fear and adrenaline, she moved, shifting awkwardly on the rough bed of hay beneath her. The ropes that bound her hands were biting into her wrists, but she could no longer focus on the pain. Her sole thought was Jamie. She had to get to him, get them both out of here.

She strained her neck, twisting awkwardly. She couldn't see her brother, but she could hear him—his ragged breathing, the soft whimpers he made whenever the fighting grew louder. The ropes around his tiny hands would be her first priority. If she could just free him, they would have a better chance of escaping whatever chaos was unfolding around them.

"Hold on, Jamie," Annalise whispered, her voice shaky but determined. "I'm gonna fix this. Just hold on, sweetheart."

The jostling of the cart grew more erratic, and she could feel Jamie's small body being tossed around like a ragdoll. He was so small, so vulnerable, and Annalise's heart cracked at the thought of him being caught in the middle of whatever was happening outside. She twisted again, trying to reach his hands behind her with her tied wrists. Her fingers brushed against the rough rope binding his hands behind his back. It was tight, but it was possible to undo if she had just enough time.

A particularly violent jolt from the cart threw her completely off-balance, nearly rolling her away from Jamie completely.

Annalise gasped as her shoulder collided with the hardwood, but she didn't stop. Through the blurred sensation of pain, she felt the rope around Jamie's wrists. Her fingers fumbled over it, the pressure building in her chest as the chaos continued to rage around them.

"Please, God," she whispered through clenched teeth, focusing all her energy on the task. "Please give me the strength to free him. Keep us safe."

She worked quickly, knowing that every moment counted. The rope was rough and the knot tight, but her hands, clumsy with fear, managed to pull it loose bit by bit. Finally, after what felt like an eternity, the knot came undone. Jamie's hands were free.

"Jamie!" she whispered urgently, "Take off the hood. Take it off quickly, and help me."

The hood was yanked off, pulling at her hair as well. She masked a hiss of pain and then Jamie's tiny hands were at her wrists, fumbling with the ropes. His movements were hesitant at first, as though he wasn't sure how to help, but soon, his fingers were working faster, pulling at the rope that bound her hands.

"Almost there," she whispered, her breath ragged. She could feel the tension in his small frame as he strained against the knot, his determination clear even if he was frightened. The urgency of the situation made her stomach turn, but she fought to remain calm for him.

"I'm proud of you, Jamie. So proud."

The knots around her wrists were loosening, and with one final tug, the rope fell away. Annalise shook her hands free, letting them fall limp at her sides for a moment to regain some feeling before she attacked the knots at her ankles, then the one around Jamie's. He threw his arms around her neck as she worked, which made it difficult, but eventually they were both free. She looked wildly around them both and saw trees flying by, men on horses near the front of the cart trying to force them to stop, and stars careening overhead in the early dawn.

"Jamie," she said, pulling his head back to make him look at her, "we need to get out of here. We're going to jump, and then we're going to run, do you understand?"

His lower lip trembled. "I don't want to jump."

"Oh, honey, I know, but we have to. It's like a game, it's like…" She stammered, jolting back and forth in the rocking cart, trying to think. "It's like the baby cows, yeah? When they jump around and run away from everyone. We're going to do that, and everything will be okay. Can you do that?"

He nodded, his little face pale. She pulled his arms away from her neck and moved them both closer to the edge of the cart, trying not to look at the rushing ground beneath.

"On my count, Jamie," she said. "One… two… three!"

She jumped. The earth rushed up to her as she landed, hard, with Jamie in her arms. She hit the ground hard and landed on her side, cupping his head to her. "Come on!" she shouted, and scrabbling up she hauled him to his feet and began to run. The fighting continued as the cart rushed off, but all Annalise could focus on was running. The trees were close—so close— and she had no intention of stopping until they were deep within the cover of the forest.

Chapter Thirty-One

The moon hung low in the sky, its pale light casting an eerie glow over the landscape. The barren fields stretched out on either side of the dirt road, the frost-covered ground shimmering faintly in the moonlight. The air was heavy with the scent of damp earth and decaying leaves, a reminder of the unforgiving winter just around the corner.

Reid's mind raced as the horses galloped onward. His jaw clenched, and his knuckles whitened as he gripped the reins tighter. The road stretched ahead of them like a dark ribbon, winding its way through sparse patches of forest and rolling hills. Reid's eyes scanned the horizon constantly, searching for any sign of movement, any clue that might lead them closer to Annalise and Jamie.

By the time they reached Carter's land, their horses were covered in lather and breathing hard. Reid barely noticed, and jumped off Lycan before he stopped completely, stomping quickly up the steps of Carter's massive, ridiculous house. He burst through the door while Wade called after him.

"Hey!" Reid shouted. "Wake up!" He grabbed an expensive looking vase and dashed it to the ground. "Wake up and talk to me before I break everything your boss owns." He moved to a painting on the wall, considering trying to get it down and smash that too before he heard footsteps racing down the halls. Servants in sleepwear appeared, looking both tired and wide awake with shock at the same time.

"Mr. Carter isn't here," one of them whispered in a voice hoarse with sleep. "There's no one here to meet with."

Reid levelled an accusing finger at the man. "There's you," he said lowly, stalking forward. The man stepped back but then Reid had him by the collar of his nightshirt. "Where did Carter go?"

"I-I... I don't know!" The man stammered, his hand trying to grab Reid's arm. "He didn't say!"

"Which direction did he set off?"

"East!" Someone else ran forward. "He was heading east; he said he'd be back before breakfast."

Reid dropped the man he was holding and turned around to leave. Wade was outside, holding Lycan's reins across his own saddle. He tossed the reins to his boss and once Reid was in the saddle, they were straight back into a gallop. "East!" Reid called over his shoulder, already heading that direction.

The sun was pushing its way into the sky as Reid and Wade galloped down the east bound road, the horses' hooves kicking up dirt and gravel. The once-cold air now carried a faint warmth, though it did nothing to ease the tension that gripped Reid's chest.

Every bend in the road, every shadow in the trees, set his nerves on edge. He leaned forward in his saddle, urging his horse to go faster. Jamie's face flashed in his mind—small, frightened, and vulnerable. And Annalise... He tried not to picture her at the mercy of Carter or the villains whose clutches he intended to sell her into, carrying the memory of her smile with him instead as he wiped the sweat from his brow.

Wade rode alongside him, his hat pulled low against the wind. "You think we're close?" he asked, shouting over the thunder of hooves.

Reid scanned the road ahead, his eyes narrowing. "We have to be," he replied, his voice tight. "They can't have gotten far with that cart."

As if on cue, the faint outline of a cart appeared in the distance, its dark shape silhouetted against the rising sun. Reid's pulse quickened.

"There," he said, pointing ahead.

Wade nodded, his face grim. "What's the plan?"

Reid's mind worked quickly. "We rush them. Spook the horses, force the cart off the road. If we're lucky, we can stop it before they know what hit them."

Wade smiled grimly, a spark of adrenaline lighting up his eyes. "Let's do it."

They urged their horses into a full gallop, the gap between them and the cart closing rapidly.

As they neared the carriage, Reid caught sight of Carter riding up front next to a driver with a rifle across his lap. In the back, the dark shape of two bodies, one an adult and one a child, was barely visible.

Reid's anger flared white-hot at the sight of them, bound and helpless.

"Stay on my left!" he shouted to Wade. "We'll cut them off!"

They veered slightly, their horses kicking up clouds of dust as they closed in on the cart. Carter glanced over his shoulder, his eyes widening in alarm as he spotted them.

"Get rid of them!" Carter shouted to the driver, his voice panicked as he grabbed the reins.

The man raised his weapon, but Wade was faster. With a sharp crack, Wade fired his revolver, the bullet whizzing past the driver's head and sending him ducking for cover.

"Stop, Carter!" Reid called out, his voice carrying over the chaos. "Pull over now!"

The horses pulling the carriage whinnied in panic, their movements erratic as Reid and Wade pressed closer. Reid urged Lycan to the side of the cart, his eyes locked on the wheel.

"Now!" he shouted.

Both men surged forward, their horses ramming against the side of the cart. The force of the impact sending the cart careening off the path. One of the wheels hit a deep ditch, the wood splintering with a loud crack.

The entire cart tipped dangerously, lurching sideways before falling back onto its wheels and continuing.. Reid cursed. "Again!" he shouted to Wade. It took time for their horses to get back into position, and both mounts hesitated as they now knew what was coming. The whole time, the cart was speeding and jolting wildly as Carter's driver tried to fire at them again and Carter himself was nearly lying down in the front seat, trying wildly to control the horses from his prone position.

They rammed the cart again, and this time it tipped over completely. Reid let out a strangled cry as the horses screamed in panic, dragging the tipped cart with them. They were supposed to stop! He could barely breathe at the thought of Jamie and Annalise being thrown from the cart or crushed beneath it. With a shout, he pushed Lycan ahead even faster until he was in front of the cart horses, then halted and turned him so he was blocking the road. The horses, tired and confused, finally slowed and eventually stopped.

Reid dismounted at once in one fluid motion, revolver drawn. His boots hit the ground hard, the impact jolting through his legs, but he barely noticed.

Carter tackled Reid with the force of a bull, driving him backward into the dirt. The impact jarred Reid's spine, but he didn't hesitate. His revolver skittered out of reach, but his fists came up instinctively. He threw a solid punch, his knuckles slamming into Carter's jaw with a satisfying crack.

Carter grunted but recovered quickly, grabbing Reid by the collar and shoving him against the side of the broken carriage. The rough wood scraped against Reid's back, but he didn't let up. He twisted sharply, breaking Carter's grip, and swung again, this time connecting with Carter's ribs.

Wade, meanwhile, had his own hands full with the driver. The two men grappled near the panicked horses, Wade managing to block a wild swing of the man's fist before landing a hard uppercut to his gut. The driver stumbled but retaliated, lunging at Wade with surprising speed.

Reid turned his attention back to Carter, who had lunged for a knife tucked into his boot. Carter slashed wildly, the blade catching the edge of Reid's coat as Reid dodged. The glint of the blade in the morning sun made Reid's heart pound faster, but his focus remained sharp.

"You're not taking them," Reid growled through clenched teeth, circling Carter.

Carter growled through bloody lips. "I can take whatever I want," he spat. "After I kill you here, I'll take your land, your cattle, your house, and I'll burn it all down!"

Reid didn't waste time on a response. He feinted left, then lunged right, grabbing Carter's knife hand. The two men struggled, their breaths labored and loud in the tense silence around them. Reid twisted Carter's wrist sharply, forcing the knife to drop into the dirt.

Carter roared in frustration, but Reid followed up with a hard elbow to his temple, sending him sprawling.

Wade managed to land another punch that sent the driver staggering, and with a final well-aimed kick to the man's shin, Wade had him down, groaning.

Reid didn't wait to catch his breath. He stepped over Carter, who was writhing on the ground, and hurried toward the back of the cart.

The dust from the crash hung heavy in the air, mingling with the tang of sweat and the earthy scent of the broken cart. Before Reid could reach the cart, a sharp metallic click froze him in place. He turned around slowly.

The cold barrel of the gun gleamed menacingly as Carter pointed it squarely at Reid's chest.

"You've got guts, I'll give you that," Carter snarled, his voice low and dripping with malice. "But guts don't mean a thing when you're dead."

Reid's breath hitched, his mind racing. His revolver was still on the ground, too far to reach without drawing Carter's fire. Wade was frozen, not wanting to get Reid shot, and the driver he'd knocked down was up and going for his rifle. Behind him, the cart creaked as it shifted slightly in the ditch, a grim reminder of the urgency of the situation.

"Carter," Reid said, his voice steady despite the pounding of his heart. "You don't want to do this. You've already crossed enough lines today. Let us go, and maybe you won't hang for it."

Carter laughed—a cold, empty sound that sent a chill down Reid's spine. "You think I'm afraid of the law? I'll just buy it, the way I buy everything. And you? You're just a speck of dust in my way."

Reid's gaze darted to Wade, who was now just glaring at the driver, who had the rifle leveled at him.

"This is insane," Reid pressed, trying to keep Carter's focus on him. "Nothing is worth this, not land or money or whatever you're after. Are you really going to kill me just to the biggest ranch in town?"

Carter's eyes narrowed, his grip tightening on the pistol. For a moment, Reid thought he'd gotten through to him. Then, without warning, Carter's finger moved toward the trigger.

A loud crack split the air, but it wasn't from Carter's gun.

Wade was grappling with the driver, his hands wrapped around the barrel of the rifle, having just barely managed to keep it from going off in his face. The distraction gave Reid the split-second he needed.

He lunged forward, slamming into Carter with every ounce of strength he had left. The gun went off, the shot ringing out like thunder as the weapon discharged into the sky. Reid wrestled Carter to the ground, their bodies hitting the dirt with a thud.

The gun tumbled from Carter's hand, landing a few feet away. Both men scrambled for it, but Reid managed to reach it first. He leveled the weapon at Carter, breathing hard. Nearby, Wade had the driver on the ground, hands on his head and the rifle pointed at him.

"It's over," Reid said, his voice firm despite the exhaustion threatening to drag him under. "Stay down." He kept the gun trained on Carter as he backed away. "Annalise! Jamie!" He called their names as he neared the toppled cart. He turned his head, trying to keep his eyes on Carter at the same time as he searched desperately for the two bodies he'd seen earlier. There was nothing but some loose rope on the dirt road. Reid growled, turning back to Carter."

"Where are they? Where are Annalise and Jamie?"

A flicker of surprise, then he shrugged. "Dead, I guess. Or run off, like she wanted. Ohh…" he grinned. "What's wrong, Shaw? Were you expecting a hero's kiss?"

Reid surged forward, hand tightening around the gun. He stopped feet away from the leering man. Wade was looking at his boss in concern, shifting uncomfortably on his feet, and Reid tried to control his breathing. "Wade," he called through gritted teeth, "tie 'em up and we'll get the sheriff and a search party out here."

The night air hung heavy with tension, the earthy scent of the forest mixing with the acrid tang of sweat and blood. Reid and Wade had barely finished tying up Carter and the driver when the sound of rustling leaves and rapid footsteps reached their ears. Reid spun, his heart pounded, each beat echoing in his chest like a drum.

And then, Carter moved.

He twisted his body with a strength born of desperation, snapping the loose binding on his wrists. Before Reid could react, Carter lunged, tackling Wade to the ground and grabbing the fallen gun.

"Stay back!" Carter snarled, holding the weapon steady as he scrambled to his feet. His wild eyes flicked between Reid and Wade. "Looks like this isn't over yet."

Reid froze, his mind racing. His own weapon was still tucked into his saddlebag, too far to retrieve. Wade groaned from where he'd been shoved to the ground, dazed but trying to rise.

Reid opened his mouth to try reasoning with Carter, but the words caught in his throat when a sudden shadow darted out from the trees. Before anyone could process what was happening, a figure leaped through the air, landing squarely on Carter's back with a force that sent the man staggering forward.

The gun clattered to the ground and slid toward Reid.

Carter cursed, his voice strangled as he tried to shake off his assailant, but the figure held on with surprising strength.

"Reid!"

The voice—familiar and desperate—pierced through Reid's haze of shock. Annalise.

She clung to Carter, her arms locked around his shoulders as she fought to keep him off balance. Carter stumbled, his knees buckling, but he twisted sharply, throwing Annalise to the ground. She landed with a gasp, the force knocking the breath from her lungs.

"Annalise!" Reid roared, his voice raw with fear and fury.

Adrenaline surged through him as he dove for the gun. His fingers closed around the cold metal just as Carter lunged again, but this time, Reid was ready.

He rolled to his feet, aiming the gun at Carter with steady hands. "Don't move," Reid commanded, his voice low and deadly.

Carter froze, his chest heaving as he glanced between the gun and Reid's unyielding expression. Behind him, Annalise pushed herself up, her face pale but determined.

Carter's gaze flickered toward the treeline as though calculating his chances of escape, but before he could act, Wade had recovered. He stood beside Reid, his stance solid despite the bruises marring his face.

"Don't even think about it," Wade warned, his voice sharp.

The other man, still tied up near the overturned cart, watched the scene unfold with wide eyes. Carter's bravado began to falter, his shoulders sagging as he realized he was out of options.

Reid took a cautious step forward, his focus unwavering. "Where's Jamie?" he asked Annalise, his voice cutting through the tense silence like a blade.

She stood on shaky legs and moved closer, her gaze locked on Carter. "He's in the woods. When I heard the commotion, I managed to escape as it was the only chance I had."

"Okay. We'll deal with these guys, and then you and Jamie can come... home." Reid looked at Annalise, and she nodded.

"Let's tie him up better this time." Wade walked forward with another rope from his saddlebag, and Reid nodded.

"Annalise, you should get Jamie," Reid said as Wade dragged and tied Carter's hands to stop him from making any other move.

Annalise hurried into the woods while Wade and Reid tied Carter to a tree.

"I haven't committed any crime," Carter sneered. "I was only returning her to where she belongs. You bought a wife from a whorehouse, you know that?"

Reid felt fury bubbling within, and he struck Carter across the face. "You should be ashamed of yourself, Carter. The Lord has told us to be kind to the weak, and yet you were taking a woman and a child to be sold. I wonder if you have any shred of humanity within you."

Annalise emerged from the woods holding Jamie's hand. "Reid," she called out.

Reid turned around and saw Jamie smiling. He ran and picked him up in his arms. "I'm so sorry, Jamie, you had to go through this." Reid looked at Annalise. "So, so sorry."

She smiled, her pale face surrounded by her hair, wild and messy. He wanted so badly to go to her and sweep her into her arms, smooth her hair and tell her that everything would be all right.

"I was afraid, but my sister said the Lord will help us." Jamie smiled, and Reid set him down.

"Wade," he called. "Wait here and keep an eye on Carter. I'll send the sheriff back to you, but first, I need to take my family home."

Epilogue

They rode back to town, Annalise and Jamie on one of the horses from the cart. Her whole body ached, and the movement of the horse didn't help, but she hugged Jamie tight to her body as she guided the horse. All the while, she kept her eyes on Reid as he rode slightly ahead of her. From time to time, he would look back at her and smile, and the pain in her body would vanish.

Once in town, Reid led them straight to the sheriff's office. She waited outside until the sheriff and his deputy emerged, hurrying towards their horses. Reid emerged, nodded, and they resumed the journey back to his house. To their *home*. Jamie's head was rapidly nodding forward, and by the time they arrived, she was squeezing him to her body so he wouldn't fall of the horse. Reid tied up the horses and took Jamie in his arms.

They both walked upstairs, and she watched as he tucked Jamie into bed. When her brother was safely down, Reid turned to her. He took her hand and led her downstairs to the kitchen table. They sat across from each other. Annalise's head was spinning from being back in the house she thought she'd never see again. It was hard to concentrate on anything with a thousand fears and hopes and thoughts swirling in her mind.

Finally, she broke the silence, her voice soft so as not to wake Jamie. "Reid… there's something I need to say."

His gaze snapped to hers, his brow furrowing in concern. "What is it, Annalise? Are you hurt?"

She shook her head quickly, her fingers tightening around Jamie's. "No, it's not that. It's just... earlier, when Carter was saying those horrible things about me, I—" She hesitated, her throat tightening. "I need you to know that I was telling the truth. About everything. I've never—" Her voice wavered, and she dropped her gaze, unable to meet his eyes. "I've never been with a man."

The words hung in the air, vulnerable and raw. Annalise held her breath, bracing for his response.

Reid leaned forward, his hands reaching across the table for hers as he fixed her with a steady, earnest look. "Annalise," he began, his voice firm yet gentle, "I never doubted you. Not for a second."

Her eyes snapped up to meet his, wide with surprise. "You... you didn't?"

He shook his head, a small smile tugging at his lips. "No. I know the kind of woman you are. Your strength, your faith—it's evident in everything you do. And I also know that God doesn't make mistakes. He brought you into my life for a reason, and I trust that with all my heart."

Tears welled in her eyes, and she blinked rapidly, her heart swelling with an emotion she couldn't quite name. "Reid, I... I've spent so much of my life feeling unworthy. Like my past would always define me. But you... you've never looked at me like that."

"That's because it's not true," he said firmly, his voice taking on an edge of conviction. "Your past doesn't define you, Annalise. It never did. And I thank God every day that He led me to you." He hesitated, his expression softening.

Her breath hitched, and she gulped, her throat too tight to speak.

Reid took a deep breath, his hands clasping together as if steeling himself for what he was about to say. "Annalise," he began, his voice steady but tinged with emotion, "I know this might not be the best time, but after everything we've been through, I can't keep this to myself any longer."

She looked at him, her heart pounding in her chest.

"I love you," he said simply, the words carrying the weight of a promise. "I've loved you from the moment I realized how brave and selfless you are. You've taught me so much about faith, about trusting in God's plan, even when it's hard to see. And I know without a doubt that you and Jamie are meant to be a part of my life."

Tears spilled over her cheeks, and she pressed a trembling hand to her lips. "Reid…"

He shifted in his seat, leaning forward as his eyes bored into hers. "I don't care about your past, Annalise. I care about who you are now and the woman you've become. And I want to spend the rest of my life with you. If you'll let me."

Her breath caught, and for a moment, all she could do was stare at him, her mind struggling to process the enormity of his words. He moved out of his seat and went on one knee beside her, clasping her hands in his.

"Annalise," he continued, his voice softening, "will you marry me? Will you let me be a part of your family, to love and protect you and Jamie for the rest of my life?"

Her heart swelled, and a sob escaped her lips as she nodded, her voice barely more than a whisper. "Yes, Reid. Yes, I'll marry you."

His radiant smile lit up his face with a joy that made her chest ache. He lifted her hand to his lips, pressing a reverent kiss to her knuckles. "You've made me the happiest man alive," he murmured.

Annalise felt a rush of warmth flood her chest, a sense of peace and belonging she hadn't felt in years. "Reid," she said softly, her voice thick with emotion, "I've prayed for so long to find a place where I belong, where Jamie and I can be safe. And now, with you... I finally feel like we've found it."

He reached up to gently cup her cheek, his thumb brushing away the tears that streaked her face. "You have, Annalise. You'll always have a home with me."

Their gazes locked, and for a moment, the world around them seemed to fade away. Reid leaned forward slowly, his movements deliberate and respectful, giving her the chance to pull away if she wanted to. But she didn't. Instead, she tilted her face toward his, her heart pounding as their lips met in a soft, tender kiss.

It wasn't a kiss born of passion or desperation but one of love and commitment, a silent promise of the life they would build together. When they finally pulled apart, their foreheads rested against each other, and Annalise let out a shaky breath.

"Thank you," she whispered, her voice trembling with emotion. "Thank you for loving me, for seeing me."

Reid smiled, his eyes shining with unshed tears. "It's easy to love you, Annalise. You're everything I've ever prayed for."

Extended Epilogue

Three Years Later

The warm afternoon sun cast a golden glow over the sprawling fairgrounds where the annual cattle auction bustled with activity. The air hummed with the sounds of lowing cattle, the chatter of ranchers, and the occasional bark of a herding dog. Reid adjusted his hat against the glare and surveyed the crowd from the edge of the pen where Jamie's prized heifer stood. Pride swelled in his chest as he watched the boy.

At eight years old, Jamie was already becoming a fine rancher. He had an instinct for animals, a patience that belied his age, and a determination that reminded Reid of Annalise. The boy's cow, a sleek, healthy young heifer with a coat like polished ebony, stood calmly as Jamie adjusted her halter.

"Hard to believe he's just a boy," Wade said, breaking Reid's thoughts. His friend stood beside him, arms crossed, as he nodded toward Jamie. "That kid handles livestock better than some men twice his age."

Reid chuckled, the sound low and satisfied. "He's got a natural talent, that's for sure. Reminds me of someone I used to know."

Wade smirked. "You mean you?"

"Maybe," Reid said, the corner of his mouth lifting. "But I wasn't nearly as polished at his age."

The auctioneer's voice rang out in the distance, sharp and rhythmic, and Reid glanced toward the large barn where the bids were underway. The fairground was alive with movement—ranchers haggling, families sharing food, and young cowboys showing off for their sweethearts. It was a scene Reid had grown up in, but seeing it through Jamie's eyes brought a new kind of joy.

"Think he's ready for this?" Wade asked, jerking his chin toward Jamie, who was now rubbing his heifer's neck and whispering to her.

"He's more than ready," Reid said, his voice firm. "He's worked hard for this moment. Annalise and I made sure he understood what it meant to bring his own cow to auction. He earned it."

Wade nodded, his expression thoughtful. "You've done right by him, Reid. That boy's lucky to have you."

Reid felt a familiar warmth in his chest at Wade's words. "I'm the lucky one. He and Annalise… they've changed my life. Gave me more than I ever thought I deserved."

Before Wade could respond, Jamie bounded over, his face alight with excitement. His sun-kissed cheeks were flushed, and his wide grin revealed a gap where a tooth had recently gone missing.

"She's ready," Jamie said, his voice brimming with pride. "I checked her again, and she's perfect. The man from down the row even said she's one of the best-looking heifers here!"

Reid ruffled Jamie's hair, his heart swelling at the boy's enthusiasm. "That's because she is, son. You've done a great job raising her."

Jamie's chest puffed out, and he looked up at Wade. "Uncle Wade, do you think she'll sell for a lot?"

Wade grinned. "If I were a betting man —and you know I am— I'd say she's going to fetch more than you expect."

Jamie's eyes sparkled, and he turned back to Reid. "Do you think Annalise will be here soon? She said she wanted to see the auction."

"She'll be here," Reid assured him, glancing toward the dirt road leading to the fairgrounds. "You know your sister wouldn't miss this for the world."

Jamie nodded, his trust in his sibling evident. "I'm glad she's coming. She always knows the right thing to say when I'm nervous."

Reid crouched down, meeting Jamie at eye level. "Nervous? There's no reason to be. You've done the work, Jamie. All that's left now is to let others see the results of it."

Jamie's smile returned, and he straightened, his small shoulders squaring with determination. "You're right, Papa. I'm ready."

Reid watched him dart back toward the pen, his heart full. The boy had taken to calling him "Papa" not long after he and Annalise married, and every time he heard the word, it reminded him of how much his life had changed in these past three years.

"He's a good kid," Wade said, breaking the momentary silence.

"The best," Reid agreed, standing once more. He scanned the crowd, his sharp eyes searching for Annalise. "And he gets it from his sister."

Wade chuckled. "That woman's made quite an impression on you."

Reid didn't deny it. "She's my anchor, Wade. My reason for everything. Seeing her and Jamie happy is all I could ever ask for."

As they talked, the hum of the auctioneer's voice grew louder, signaling the next round of bids. Jamie's heifer would be up soon, and Reid couldn't wait to see the boy's face when his hard work was recognized.

Suddenly, a flash of blue caught his eye, and Reid turned to see Annalise walking toward them. She wore a simple dress that swayed gently with each step, her hat shading her face from the sun. Their nearly two-year-old daughter, Lily, was perched on her hip, her tiny hands clutching at the brim of Annalise's hat. Her wide blue eyes darted around, taking in everything with the wonder only a child could muster.

Reid stepped forward, meeting Annalise halfway. She stopped before him, her eyes sparkling with love and pride. "I hear we've got a future cattleman making waves around here," she teased, glancing toward Jamie.

"We sure do," Reid said, his voice softening as he reached for her free hand. "And he's got the best role model anyone could ask for."

Annalise laughed, a sound that always reminded Reid of hope and home. "I think he gets his determination from you."

Reid shook his head. "That boy's got his own fire. I just help keep it burning."

She squeezed his hand, her expression growing tender. "You've done more than that, Reid. You've given him a home, a family. And you've shown him what it means to be loved."

His throat tightened, and he brought her hand to his lips, brushing a kiss across her knuckles. "He's given me just as much, Annalise. Both of you have."

Their moment was interrupted by Jamie's excited shout. "Annalise! You're here!"

Annalise turned, her smile widening as Jamie ran toward her. She crouched to embrace him, her arms wrapping around him tightly. "I wouldn't miss it for the world. Are you ready?"

Jamie nodded, pulling back to look up at her. "Papa says she's the best heifer here."

"Well," Annalise said, her tone playful, "if your papa says so, it must be true."

"Cow!" Lily announced loudly, pointing a chubby finger toward Jamie's heifer. Her little voice rang out clear and bright over the hum of the auction grounds. "Black cow!"

Annalise chuckled, shifting Lily higher on her hip. "That's right, sweetheart. It's a black cow. And what about that one?" She nodded toward a nearby pen where a brown-and-white speckled steer grazed lazily.

"Brown cow!" Lily proclaimed, bouncing slightly in Annalise's arms as though the discovery thrilled her.

Reid strode forward, his grin broadening. "She's getting pretty good at naming animals," he said as he reached them, brushing a hand over Lily's soft curls.

Annalise's smile was warm, her gaze meeting his with the familiar light that always made him feel like the most fortunate man alive. "She's had plenty of practice on the ranch," she said. "Though she did call one of the sheep a cow last week."

Reid laughed, low and deep, the sound mixing with the murmur of the crowd. "Well, give her time. By the looks of it, she's already got an eye for livestock."

Lily reached for him, her small hands opening and closing with urgency. "Papa!"

"Come here, darlin'," Reid said, lifting her into his arms with ease. Her tiny fingers immediately grabbed at his shirt as she settled against him, her head resting on his shoulder.

"Papa, black cow," she said again as if making sure he understood.

"I see it, Lily," he replied, his voice softening. "That's your brother's cow. He worked hard to bring her here today."

"Jamie's cow," Lily repeated, her pronunciation slightly garbled but earnest. Reid chuckled, his chest tightening with affection.

Annalise stepped closer, adjusting the brim of her hat to shield her face from the sun. "She's been talking about this all morning," she said. "I think she's more excited than Jamie."

"Hard to imagine," Reid said, glancing toward Jamie, who was now animatedly explaining the auction process to one of the other young ranchers. "That boy's been counting down the days. You should've heard him this morning, making sure every hair on that cow was in place."

Annalise laughed softly, her eyes drifting toward Jamie. "He's growing up so fast. It feels like just yesterday we were trying to convince him he didn't have to sleep with his boots on."

Reid smiled at the memory, his hand brushing lightly against hers. "He's turning into a fine young man. And it's thanks to you."

Her gaze snapped to his, startled. "Me?"

"Yes, you," he said firmly. "You've given him a home where he feels safe and loved. You've taught him what it means to be strong and kind. I just help steer the ship."

Annalise's eyes softened, and she reached out to place a hand on his arm. "You do more than steer, Reid. You've given him something no one else ever could—a father's love. He's thriving because of you."

Reid felt his throat tighten, and he glanced away briefly, the weight of her words settling over him. When he looked back, he saw nothing but sincerity in her gaze. "It's not just him," he said quietly. "You've given me a reason to wake up every day and be better. Both of you." He nodded toward Lily, who was now inspecting the buttons on his shirt with deep concentration.

"And her?" Annalise asked, her voice teasing. "What's she taught you?"

"That I've got my hands full," he said with a grin, eliciting a laugh from Annalise. He bent his head to kiss Lily's temple, her giggle warm against his cheek. "But I wouldn't trade it for the world."

Lily suddenly leaned back, her small hand reaching out toward her mother. "Mama," she said insistently.

"Looks like I'm needed," Annalise said, taking Lily back into her arms. The toddler immediately rested her head against her mother's shoulder, her eyes already beginning to droop from the excitement of the day.

"Looks like someone's ready for a nap," Reid said, brushing a finger gently against Lily's cheek.

Annalise smiled, her expression soft and full of love. "It's been a big day for her."

Reid stepped closer, his voice dropping slightly so only Annalise could hear. "It's been a big day for all of us. I know we've been through a lot, but seeing you here, holding our little girl... I couldn't have dreamed of a better life."

Annalise's eyes glistened, and she tilted her head toward his shoulder briefly, a simple gesture that spoke volumes. "God's been good to us," she said quietly.

Reid nodded, his heart full. "He has. More than I could ever deserve."

They stood together, the fairgrounds bustling around them, but in that moment, the world felt still. As Reid watched Annalise sway gently with Lily in her arms, he was struck again by the enormity of the blessings he'd been given—a loving wife, a thriving son, and a future that felt limitless.

"Jamie's cow," Lily murmured sleepily, her tiny voice drawing a laugh from both Reid and Annalise.

"That's right, darlin'," Reid said softly. "Jamie's cow. And your papa couldn't be prouder."

***

The crowd at the auction had thinned as the afternoon wore on, leaving a more relaxed air in its wake. Annalise sat with Laura on a bench near the edge of the fairgrounds, the low hum of voices and the occasional bawl of cattle serving as background music to their conversation.

The late afternoon sun cast a warm golden glow over everything, softening the edges of the bustling auction and creating an intimate cocoon around the two women.

Annalise leaned back, tucking a stray strand of hair behind her ear as she watched Lily toddle after Jamie, who was carefully showing her how to identify different kinds of cattle. Laura followed her gaze, a soft smile tugging at her lips.

"You've got yourself quite the pair there," Laura said, nodding toward the children. "Jamie's growing up to be a fine young man, and Lily—well, she's going to have every rancher wrapped around her little finger before long."

Annalise chuckled. "She already does. She's got Reid tied in knots, though he'd never admit it."

Laura laughed, the sound light and genuine. "Oh, I believe it. There's nothing quite like a little girl to soften even the toughest of men."

They fell into a comfortable silence, both women watching the children with matching expressions of quiet contentment. After a moment, Annalise turned to Laura, her tone thoughtful. "I don't think I ever thanked you properly."

Laura raised an eyebrow, her smile fading slightly. "For what?"

"For everything," Annalise said simply. "For trying to help me. And for standing up to Carter, even when it would've been easier to stay quiet."

Laura's expression softened, and she reached over to place a hand on Annalise's arm. "You don't owe me any thanks, Annalise. If anything, I should be thanking you. You gave me the courage to step up and take control of my life. Watching you fight for your family, for your freedom—it reminded me that I could do the same."

Annalise shook her head. "You've done so much more than that. Look at what you've built, Laura. Carter's ranch wasn't just saved; you turned it into something remarkable. You earned the respect of everyone who ever doubted you."

Laura smiled, a hint of pride in her expression. "I'll admit, it wasn't easy. There were days I wanted to throw in the towel, especially in the beginning. But every time I thought about giving up, I thought about you. About how you never let fear stop you. And that gave me the strength to keep going."

Annalise's eyes glistened, and she blinked quickly, glancing away. "I don't know how I would've gotten through it all without you. You were my friend when I felt like I didn't have anyone."

"You always had someone," Laura said gently. "You just didn't see it at the time. God has a way of placing people in our lives exactly when we need them."

Annalise nodded, her gaze distant for a moment as she reflected on those difficult days. "I used to think everything I went through was a punishment. That I'd made too many mistakes and this was my way of paying for them. But now..."

She smiled softly, her eyes flicking to where Reid was now helping Jamie load a small pen gate onto the wagon. "Now I see that it was all part of His plan. If I hadn't gone through those trials, I wouldn't be here. I wouldn't have Reid or the children. And I wouldn't have found my strength."

Laura nodded, her own eyes misting. "It's funny, isn't it? How life takes us to places we never imagined. I never thought I'd be running a ranch, let alone thriving at it. And yet, here we are."

Annalise smiled. "Here we are."

They sat in silence again, the weight of their shared history and hard-earned victories hanging in the air like a tangible thing.

Laura broke the quiet, her tone turning lighter. "Speaking of thriving, have you given any thought to hosting that harvest festival you mentioned last year? I think it's about time this town celebrated something other than cattle auctions."

Annalise laughed, the sound bright and warm. "Reid's been after me about it, too. He says the barn would make a perfect venue. I think he just wants an excuse to show off his woodworking skills."

"Whatever the reason, I say we do it," Laura said firmly. "I'll help you plan it. Between the two of us, we can make it the event of the season."

"You're on," Annalise said with a grin.

The two women shared a laugh, the sound carrying on the breeze as the sun dipped lower in the sky. It was a moment of peace and connection, a reminder of how far they'd come and the bond that had carried them through it all. Together, they were stronger than they ever could've been alone, and they both knew it.

***

Two hours later, Annalise stood near one of the large pens, her hands resting lightly on the railing as she watched Laura handle negotiations with a pair of ranchers. Laura had always carried herself with confidence, but now, there was an edge of self-assured authority that Annalise couldn't help but admire. Dressed in a practical riding skirt and a crisp blouse, her hat tilted just enough to shield her from the sun, Laura looked every bit the rancher she'd become.

The transformation was remarkable. After Carter's arrest, Laura had faced an uphill battle, stepping into a world that had long dismissed her as little more than a trophy wife. Carter's men had been wary at first, skeptical of her abilities and unwilling to follow her lead. But Laura had proved them wrong. She'd worked alongside them, day and night, showing she wasn't afraid to get her hands dirty or make tough decisions. Slowly but surely, she'd earned their respect and solidified her place as the leader of her former husband's ranch.

"Ten head for fifty dollars apiece, and you've got a deal," Laura said firmly, crossing her arms as she addressed the two men.

The older of the two ranchers scratched his chin, his brows knitting together as he considered. "Fifty's steep."

Laura arched a brow, unflinching. "Then find someone else who'll offer you cattle with this quality for less. But I'll tell you right now, you won't."

The younger rancher chuckled, nudging his partner. "She's got you there, Sam."

Sam grumbled but extended his hand. "All right, Miss Laura. You've got yourself a deal."

Laura clasped his hand firmly, her smile both professional and triumphant. "Pleasure doing business with you."

As the men walked away, Laura turned to Annalise with a grin. "Some of them still think they can sweet-talk me into lowering my prices. But they're learning."

"They'd be fools to underestimate you," Annalise said warmly.

Before Laura could respond, Reid approached, his steps purposeful but relaxed. Lily was nestled against his shoulder, fast asleep, her tiny fingers clutching the fabric of his shirt. He paused next to Annalise, his free hand brushing her arm in a small but affectionate gesture.

"You're popular today, Laura," he remarked, nodding toward the departing ranchers.

Laura laughed. "It's the cattle, not me. Though I'll admit, it feels good to see all this hard work paying off."

Reid smiled, his gaze flicking to Annalise. "Hard work has a way of doing that."

Laura's expression turned mischievous as she glanced between them. "Speaking of hard work, you two could use a break. Go stretch your legs and take in the fairgrounds. I'll watch the children."

Jamie, overhearing, scoffed. "I don't need a nurse, Miss Laura."

Laura grinned at him. "Of course not, Jamie. But someone's got to keep an eye on you while you keep an eye on the cattle."

Reid chuckled, his voice warm. "You're sure you don't mind?"

"Not at all," Laura said, waving them off. "Go on. I've got this."

Annalise hesitated, glancing at Lily's sleeping form. "She's a handful when she wakes up."

Laura tilted her head, her expression fond. "I think I can handle a toddler. Besides, Jamie will keep her entertained, won't you, Jamie?"

Jamie puffed out his chest. "Of course."

With that, Laura shooed them away, herding Jamie toward the pen where his heifer was kept. Reid and Annalise exchanged a glance, and he extended his arm toward her. "Shall we?"

Annalise slipped her hand into the crook of his elbow, letting him guide her away from the bustling auction. The sun was warm, and the air carried the earthy scent of livestock and fresh hay. For a moment, it felt like the world had slowed, leaving them in their own quiet bubble.

They wandered toward the edge of the auction grounds, where the crowd's noise faded into a gentle hum. Reid led them to a shaded patch beneath a cluster of trees, their branches swaying lightly in the breeze. He turned to face her, his expression thoughtful.

"You've been busy," he said, his tone teasing. "Between chasing Lily and keeping up with Jamie, you're running circles around the rest of us."

Annalise laughed softly. "It's a lot, but I wouldn't trade it for anything. Watching Jamie grow into such a fine young man... seeing Lily discover the world... it's a blessing, Reid."

"It is," he agreed, his voice low. He reached for her hand, lacing his fingers through hers. "And none of it would've been possible without you."

She tilted her head, her eyes searching his. "You give me too much credit."

"Not enough," he countered. "Annalise, you've been my anchor. My partner. Everything I didn't know I needed."

Her cheeks flushed, but she held his gaze, her heart swelling at his words. "And you've been mine, Reid. More than I ever thought I deserved."

He lifted her hand to his lips, brushing a kiss across her knuckles. "I'm grateful every day for the life we've built together. For you."

They stood in silence for a moment, the weight of their journey together settling over them. Annalise leaned into him, resting her head against his chest, where his heartbeat thrummed steady and strong beneath her ear.

"We've come a long way," she murmured.

"We have," he said softly, his arms wrapping around her. "And I wouldn't change a thing."

THE END

Also, by Chloe Carley

Thank you for reading "**Finding Grace on His Ranch** "!

I hope you enjoyed it! If you did, here are some of my other books!

Best sellers of mine:

#1 A Surprise Bride for the Cowboy's Christmas

#2 Finding Forgiveness in the West

#3 A Godsent Governess for the Reserved Rancher

#4 Shedding God's Light on his Broken Heart

or check my Boxsets:

#1 Three Unlucky Brides on their Miraculous Paths

#2 Three Faithful Heavenly Brides

#3 Three Brides' Praying Misfits

#4 Three Daring Matches Made in Heaven

Also, if you liked this book, you can also check out my full Amazon Book Catalogue at: https://go.chloecarley.com/bc-authorpage

Thank you for allowing me to keep doing what I love! ♥

Printed in Dunstable, United Kingdom

69211148R00143